DATA LOOKED PUZZLED . . .

"Have we met, sir?"

A cold wind blew through Picard. He shot Data a look and said with exaggerated care, "This is Professor Baldwin. We picked him up on Tantamon Four. You escorted him from the transporter room."

"I did?" Data asked.

"You did," said Picard. Baldwin and Shubunkin looked at the captain, mystified.

"Something wrong?" Shubunkin asked.

"Very wrong," Picard replied. "As you may know, Data is an android. He's never forgotten anything before . . ."

Look for STAR TREK Fiction from Pocket Books

Star Trek: The Original Series

#17

STAR TREK®
THE NEXT GENERATION™

BOOGEYMEN

MEL GILDEN

POCKET BOOKS

New York   London   Toronto   Sydney   Tokyo   Singapore

An *Original* Publication of POCKET BOOKS

POCKET BOOKS, a division of Simon & Schuster Inc.
1230 Avenue of the Americas, New York, NY 10020

STAR TREK is a Registered Trademark of
® Paramount Pictures.

This book is published by Pocket Books, a division of
Simon & Schuster Inc., under exclusive license from
Paramount Pictures.

ISBN: 0-671-70970-4

First Pocket Books printing July 1991

10 9 8 7 6 5 4 3 2 1

POCKET and colophon are registered trademarks of
Simon & Schuster Inc.

Printed in the U.S.A.

For Marc and Elaine Zicree:
Just a couple of space cadets

The poem that Captain Picard recites to Wesley is by Victorian poet James Thomson (1834–1882).

BOOGEYMEN

Prologue

Wesley Crusher's Personal Log, Stardate 43747.3:
I don't seem to be making any progress in my pre-commission course. I'm proficient in science or math, anything for which logical thinking is all that's needed. But when it comes to command, I don't know if I have what in the twentieth century they called "the right stuff."

Commander Riker tells me that being a good commander is at least half intuition. Generally, the more important a question is, the less data you have available to answer it. He says that the skills one uses to decide correctly are more likely to be learned playing poker than chess. Maybe it's too bad I'm such a good chess player.

Commander Riker assures me that even Captain Picard, who likes to do things by the Starfleet book, is as successful as he is only because he knows when to ignore the book and go with his gut feelings.

He expects the unexpected. When I told Data about this, he said that expecting the unexpected was, by definition, impossible. Sometimes Data is too literal to get the point.

What about Data? Being a machine, he has no intuition. At least, that's what he tells me. But he is a *very complex* machine, and the vast number of circuits in his positronic brain—a number that approaches the number of synapses in a human brain—allows him to manifest behavior that sometimes *looks* like intuitive thinking. Are appearance and reality ever the same thing? How do you know? Not Mom or Riker or Geordi or even Data can give me a satisfactory answer.

Therefore I have to believe it's possible to *learn* to be intuitive. Or, if I can't do that, maybe I can gain so much experience that it will *look* like intuition. But how can I get experience running a starship? I had a hard time convincing Captain Picard that I belong on the bridge. What are my chances of convincing him that I should sit in the center seat? I have two chances—slim and none. (That's kind of a joke. I'll have to see if Data understands it. He always appreciates an opportunity to understand humor, even when he fails.)

Leaving the *Enterprise* and going to Starfleet Academy is out of the question. I'll have to go eventually, but right now—

"MR. CRUSHER to the bridge." It was Commander Riker's voice, and Wesley smiled.

Enterprise had entered the Omega Triangulae region three days before, searching for the source of a signal that possibly was being broadcast by an unknown intelligent race. The signal was too ordered and repetitive to be natural. Its origin was more a cloud than a point source, and it seemed to move. At the moment, specialists were taking sensor scans, doing the dull grunt work of which most exploration consisted. Commander Riker had promised to call Wesley if they found anything interesting.

Excitedly, Wesley touched his insignia and said, "I'm on my way." He touched a pad on the recorder, ejecting the isolinear chip on which he was recording his personal log, and ran from his room.

Captain Jean-Luc Picard watched the main screen intently, though at the moment nothing was on it but deep space. His mind drifted from the object of their search and Mr. Data's constant updates to the hard, cold beauty of space itself. He always found deep space to be hypnotic, which was one of the reasons he'd joined Starfleet, perhaps the main one.

Earth psychologists had defined a mental state they called rapture of the deeps. Originally it described the euphoria one felt when looking into a very large, deep hole such as North America's Grand Canyon. The euphoria was even stronger in space; recruits needed to constantly fight the urge to leap through the main viewscreen and into the vastness beyond. In a limited number of cases smashed noses had been the result of someone losing control.

To Picard's right sat Commander William Riker, his number one. Riker narrowed his eyes and nodded in answer to some private question. He had a temper and could be too quick to judge, but he also had an analytical mind second to that of few humans, so his judgments were generally correct. As for his temper, well, lesser men had mastered worse things.

On his left was Counselor Deanna Troi, wearing one of the blue, barely regulation gowns she preferred. She seemed to be the most relaxed person on the bridge, though her wide questioning eyes showed a profound interest in what was going on. Her job was to report her empathic feelings in situations in which little hard data was available. Her empathy occasionally crossed the line into sympathy, but that was not necessarily a defect. In some instances, it could even be a boon. She was a resource that Picard appreciated.

Data called out, "Object closing at warp six. Estimated time to contact, seven point four three minutes."

"Prepare to intercept, Mr. Winston-Smyth," Riker said.

"Aye, sir." The blond woman touched a pad on the conn panel.

Picard looked in the direction of the aft turbolift as its doors hissed open. "Take the conn, please, Mr. Crusher."

"Aye, sir." Wesley walked quickly to his station while Ensign Winston-Smyth slid out of the way and took up a position at mission ops, directly behind Lieutenant Worf.

Data cocked his head and said, "This is very odd, sir." He changed a setting on his board. "The object is moving at warp six, but there is no evidence that a warp drive is being employed."

A voice behind Picard said, "We are dealing with aliens, Commander. Anything is possible. Anything not forbidden by the rules of the universe is eventually required." It was a deep voice, almost lugubrious in tone.

Picard did not turn around. He knew that standing next to Worf was a Starfleet lieutenant named Shubunkin. Shubunkin was a first contact specialist. Early in the history of the Federation, races had just blundered into each other. Inevitably, mistakes in protocol, etiquette, and courtesy were made. The result was frequently bad feeling or even war—breaches that could take years to repair. Specialists were needed to soften the shock of meeting.

"It seems to me," said Riker as he looked over his shoulder at Lieutenant Shubunkin, "that there's no need to be unnecessarily mysterious or metaphysical about this. Aliens do things differently from us. That's what makes them alien."

Picard did not dare smile. His first officer was as open-minded as any officer in Starfleet, but that did not prevent him from needling Shubunkin for his pretension.

"I can pick up the object on visual now," Data said.

"Do so," said Picard.

The image wavered and then, in the center of the screen, Picard saw a sliver of brightness that was not a star. It was too big and the wrong shape.

"Magnification five," said Riker.

When the image re-formed, the screen showed a

kind of ship Picard had never before seen. It seemed to have no engines, no sensors, no windows, nothing to break its smooth silvery surface.

"It looks like a teardrop," Riker said.

"An apt description, sir," Data said. "It is likely that the streamlined shape means the ship was designed for use in atmosphere as well as in space. It is also the source of the broadcasts we have come to investigate."

Data touched his control pad, and the signal came up on audio: it sounded like insects playing insect musical instruments. The signal had no melody that Picard could discern; computer analysis confirmed his conclusion. Yet the sounds were pleasant, even relaxing. Who was making them and what did they mean?

"That will be enough, Mr. Data."

"Aye, sir." The audio repeat of the signal stopped, though Picard knew it was being recorded and analyzed deep in the bowels of the main computer.

Wesley licked his lips. He never took his eyes off the viewscreen. He had listened hard to the transmission, as if he could wring some meaning from it that the computer could not. And perhaps Wesley could. Picard liked the boy as well as he liked anyone he considered a child. Wesley was intelligent and creative —if a little overeager and entirely lacking in experience. Someday he might even become a good Starfleet officer.

Riker said, "Can you tell us what's aboard, Data?"

Sitting behind Data, Picard could see by the way his head jerked and his spine straightened that something

6

had astonished him. Data was an android, but he had been around humans for so long he could not help acquiring their habits. As a matter of fact, he worked hard at learning them. Like Pinocchio, Data wanted to be a real boy. He said, "Sensors indicate two discrete groups of beings. The members of one group are within two percentage points of being human. Members of the other"—his hands played across his ops board—"are so alien that the Federation has no category for them." He touched a pad and then went on. "Temperature, pressure, and composition of the atmosphere are well within Earth norms. Brain wave patterns and activity levels indicate that the humanoids are asleep."

"'Curiouser and curiouser,'" Picard said. "Any evidence of warp engines?"

"Sensors show a large output of energy from a structure that fills the tail of the ship, but how the energy is being generated and what is being done with it is unknown. However . . ."

"Yes, Mr. Data?" Riker said.

"Small fluctuations in the energy output match within two percentage points similar fluctuations in the brain activity of the humanoids."

Lieutenant Shubunkin said, "Very interesting."

They had picked up Shubunkin at Starbase 123 a month before. Since that time, Picard had come to sympathize with Riker's dislike for the man's attitude of smug superiority. There was no question he knew his subject, but Shubunkin got on Picard's nerves. The crew of a starship was a family. Each had to act for the benefit of all the others. There was no room for purposely ostentatious displays of any kind. Politely, Picard said, "You've seen this sort of thing before?"

"No, never. It is interesting nonetheless."

"Quite true," Picard said. He allowed himself to be pleased that there was a limit to Shubunkin's knowledge.

"Telepathic control is a possibility," Shubunkin said without certainty.

Troi said, "I am receiving no impressions of rational thought." She put a hand to her forehead. "The feelings are confused, but I am certain the beings aboard the ship mean us no harm. I feel curiosity, perhaps, and some fear—probably of us."

"How can they fear us?" Worf said. "If they have no sensors, they can't even know we exist."

"I remind you they are going at warp speed without warp engines," Data said.

Riker nodded and said, "Where are the other aliens?"

"Sensors cannot pinpoint them exactly," Data said. He sounded confused and a little dismayed.

Picard said, "Opinions, Lieutenant Shubunkin?"

"I don't have enough data at the moment to make an informed guess. I suggest we wait and see what is done by the ship or its crew. Doing nothing is frequently our wisest action."

Riker looked at Picard, eyebrows up. Picard said, "All stop, Mr. Crusher." To Riker he said, "Let them come to us. If we must do nothing, let it work in our favor."

"Shall I ready phasers, Captain?" Worf said.

Shubunkin said, "If they have sensors after all, that would not be considered a friendly act."

"Stay alert, Mr. Worf," Picard said.

Worf growled and said, "Aye, sir."

As the alien ship approached the *Enterprise*, it slowed to sublight speed and soon was creeping along at a few thousand meters per second.

"I guess this is about as unexpected as it gets," Wesley said.

"At any rate," Data said, "*I* was not expecting a ship such as this. Of course, the nature of reality is such that expectations are frequently dashed. For instance, I did not expect to meet Lieutenant La Forge in the corridor this morning. I did not expect Commander Riker to win at poker last night. I did not expect him to—"

"That will be all, Mr. Data," Riker said.

"Aye, sir," said Data, looking as if he had not expected that interruption.

The alien ship slowed even more and stopped little more than a kilometer away. It did all this without Data being able to detect a propulsion system of any kind or a way to navigate. Time went by. Picard realized that he was leaning forward in his chair. He relaxed against the backrest and settled his hands in his lap. Air circulated in a whisper. Machines made their small birdlike noises as they worked. His command crew fidgeted, all but Mr. Data. He could sit without moving for hours if necessary, though Picard always found the sight unnerving.

"How long do you suggest we do nothing, Lieutenant Shubunkin?" Riker asked in a tone that was not quite sarcastic.

Before Shubunkin or anybody else had a chance to speak, a teeth-jarring whine began. It seemed to come from all around them. Like the others, Picard covered his ears, but the sound went right through his hands. Data and Worf checked readings on their boards.

Worf called out, "An energy beam has penetrated our navigational shields."

"Analyze and identify," Riker said.

A moment later Data said, "I believe we are being subjected to a very powerful but primitive sensor scan. As it passes through the walls of the ship, unfocused fringe energy stimulates their molecules to vibrate at a high frequency."

"Shields, Mr. Worf," Picard said.

The whine did not change.

"Ineffective, Captain," Data said. "However, changing the frequency of our shield generators may . . ." His hands played across the ops board. The whine stopped as suddenly as it had begun.

"Thank you, Mr. Data," Picard said.

"Thanks are inappropriate, sir. We are no longer being scanned."

"Open hailing frequencies. Broadcast universal greetings and peace messages."

"Aye, sir," Worf said as he complied.

"Waiting—" Shubunkin began.

A little angrily, Picard said, "Perhaps they are waiting for *us.*"

A long moment later Worf said, "No response of any kind, sir."

"Continue broadcasting peace messages. Number One, ready an away team."

Commander Riker barely had time to acknowledge Picard's order before the alien ship moved to the other edge of the viewscreen without passing through the space in between. It was just suddenly *there.*

"Belay that order, Number One."

Shubunkin walked forward and stood at the end of the tactical rail.

"Incredible," Wesley cried out.

Picard said, "Incredible indeed, Mr. Crusher. Would anyone care to comment further?"

Lieutenant Shubunkin said, "As I suspected, they've seen our peace messages as a hostile intrusion."

The alien ship jumped again. It hopped toward the *Enterprise* and then away. "That is not the action of a being who is ready either to fight or to retreat," Picard said. "It is acting more like a playful kitten."

"The reason we cannot see them move," Data said, "is that they are hopping from place to place at warp speed."

Wesley said, "Using the warp drive to move such short distances is a tremendous waste of energy."

"It would certainly be a tremendous waste of energy to use *our* warp engines that way," Data said. "Moving with that precision would also require a control system many generations beyond the one aboard the *Enterprise.*"

"I believe the greetings and peace messages were understood to be an attempt at communication," Troi said. "Captain Picard's comparison of the ship's movements to those of a kitten are quite apt."

Picard said, "Then I suggest we dangle a bit of string in front of it. Lieutenant?" Picard glanced in Shubunkin's direction.

"Perhaps," Shubunkin said, and stroked his chin.

"Mr. Crusher, ahead dead slow."

"Aye, sir."

Picard watched the alien ship closely as it grew larger in the viewscreen. Somehow he had to prod the crew or the ship's automatic systems to respond in some way to the presence of the *Enterprise*. He was certain that not even an expert like Shubunkin could communicate with a being who would not communicate back.

Eventually Picard would attempt to take the ship onto a shuttle deck and allow Lieutenant Shubunkin to study it at close range. But that would be a last resort. For now the ship had a right to act in a way that made no sense to him. It was the nature of aliens to act in an alien manner. To see such things was another reason Picard had gone into space.

The alien ship stopped hopping. Picard got the impression it was watching their approach, but that was only fancy. Even if those aboard really were watching the approach of the *Enterprise,* Picard had no way of knowing it. Then, so fast that it left a momentary smudge on the viewscreen, the ship was gone. Picard blinked at the empty field of stars.

"Warp six," Data said. "Heading one four seven mark four. Still no evidence of a warp engine. But the ship continues to broadcast its signal."

"Warp six, Mr. Crusher," Riker said. "Take your heading from Mr. Data."

"Aye, sir."

The stars flew to the edges of the viewscreen, always fed by more at the center. The *Enterprise* seemed to be flinging itself down an infinitely long tunnel that had sparks embedded in its obsidian walls.

"Heading two seven six mark eight."

Wesley made the proper adjustment.

The alien ship went to warp eight, dropped back to warp five, and changed its direction three more times.

Counselor Troi yelped. A second later Data said, "The ship is gone."

"Explain," said Picard.

"Just gone, sir. It was there and then it was not."

Troi composed herself and smiled shyly. "I felt it leaving, sir."

"Felt it?" Riker said.

Troi nodded. "A pressure I didn't even know was there was suddenly gone." She thought for a moment. "It tickled when it slipped away."

Picard frowned and glanced at Riker, who gave a tiny shrug.

Data said, "The feelings that Counselor Troi describes closely approximate the event as seen by the sensors. The ship slipped away. But in a direction the sensors are not equipped to recognize and with which I am not familiar."

"Subspace?" Picard said. "Hyperspace?"

"Unknown at this time, Captain."

"Can you make sense of this, Lieutenant Shubunkin?" Picard said.

Shubunkin said, "No, sir. But I'm sure a few hours with the sensor log will—"

Picard said, "All the facilities of the ship are open to you."

"Perhaps you would like Mr. Data to assist?" Riker said.

"No, no. I just need a few hours alone with the raw data." He smiled. "Small *d.*"

Shubunkin left the bridge, and Captain Picard invited Data and Troi to join him in his ready room. They could tell him no more than what was already obvious: the signal was sent by aliens who could travel at warp speed without a warp drive; the aliens were human or they were not.

"It is all very odd," Picard said.

Data and Troi could only agree.

Shubunkin did not emerge from his stateroom for the rest of the day. And when he did appear at last, he still had no answers for Picard.

The *Enterprise* patrolled the Omega Triangulae region for another week. Everyone was disappointed that no more inexplicable events occurred, though as Wesley commented, "The mystery we already have is a doozy."

Chapter One

CAPTAIN WESLEY CRUSHER of the starship *Enterprise* brooded as he watched the Romulan captain on the main screen. Negotiations had not been going well and the diplomatic language had worn a little thin. Next to Crusher, Commander Riker was sweating heavily.

Captain Arvak shook his head and said, "I am not convinced, Crusher, that the Federation is negotiating in good faith."

Crusher opened his hands in the universal gesture of friendship, and smiled. He said, "I assure you, Captain Arvak, that given a chance the Federation would be pleased to *share* the riches of Regan Three."

"Your assurances mean nothing," Arvak said. "We have nothing more to discuss." The screen went blank, and a moment later Mr. Worf sang out, "Three Romulan ships closing fast."

"Tactical, Mr. Worf," Captain Crusher said calmly.

On the main screen, *Enterprise* was a blue dot at the center of a three-dimensional grid. The Romulan vessels were red sparks closing fast.

"Mr. Worf, sound red alert. Mr. Winston-Smyth, ahead full impulse."

The Klaxon sounded. Lights flashed. All decks reported in. Captain Crusher felt a hot adrenaline rush as he gripped the arms of his command chair. The Romulans were making it difficult for the *Enterprise* to escape without killing or being killed, but Crusher would do his best. He did not want three weeks of careful negotiations to go to waste.

"We're dead men," Riker grumbled.

Data called, "Five hundred thousand klicks and closing."

"Visual," Captain Crusher said.

The tactical display on the main screen dissolved into the view forward. The Romulan ships seemed to be right off *Enterprise*'s bow. Crusher knew the proximity of the Romulan ships was only an illusion, but he also knew they were too close for comfort.

A spot on the center Romulan ship flashed and a photon torpedo whirled toward them.

"Shields," Crusher said.

Enterprise rocked with the impact of the torpedo. The bridge lights dimmed momentarily.

"Minor damage on deck six," Worf said. "Shields still intact."

Data said, "Romulans now at sublight. Speed falling. Stabilizing at one-half impulse. Ten thousand klicks and closing."

"Tactical," Crusher demanded. The blips representing the two flank vessels peeled off to either side while the center one came ahead under a barrage of phaser fire. Crusher knew what the Romulans had in mind. It was an old trick. While one ship kept him busy at his bow, the other two would close in on both sides, concentrating their fire on his warp nacelles, hoping to destroy the propulsion coils.

"We must do something, Captain," Riker said. He sounded desperate.

"Wait, wait," Crusher said. He never took his eyes off the tactical display. He said, "Mr. Winston-Smyth, on my command, full impulse power heading zero one five mark four."

Winston-Smyth glanced worriedly at Crusher but said, "Aye, sir," and laid in the velocity.

"Wait. Wait. Wait." He cried, "Now, Mr. Winston-Smyth."

The tactical display showed *Enterprise* rising straight up. The Romulan ships were left scrambling among themselves. "Warp eight back to Federation space," Crusher said steadily.

Riker shook his head and said, "You're a man of iron nerves, sir."

Crusher nodded and smiled sardonically. Though he had failed as a diplomat, he'd managed to escape from the Romulans without inflicting or sustaining damage. Considering the Romulans, that was a victory of sorts. Yet something was missing. The element of surprise, perhaps. It was always so predictable. Not like in the real universe. He shook his head and said, "Number One, you have the bridge." He strode to the door and into his ready room, where he sat down at his desk and rested his chin on his fists.

It wasn't Guinan's fault he wasn't satisfied, or his

mom's either. Mom was swell, and Wesley liked her a lot. Still, she was a Starfleet officer mostly because she was a doctor; when it came to actually being a command officer—well, she'd never been to command school, and she did not have the experience Wesley felt he needed to call upon. He'd been a little nervous about going to Will Riker or anybody else on the bridge. They'd help him, of course, but he asked them enough questions. And they might think his request was out of line or, worse yet, silly.

So he'd gone to Guinan.

It was ship's day, so Ten Forward was nearly empty. An off-duty couple spoke low in a corner. Guinan was behind the bar wiping it down with a purple rag the same color as her dress and hat. She smiled warmly when she saw him—she did everything warmly—and said, "Taking a study break?"

"Sort of," Wesley said. He sat down and did not meet her eyes.

"What'll you have?" Guinan said.

"A clear ether, please."

While Guinan spritzed soda into a tall glass, she said, "What's wrong?"

"What makes you think something is wrong?" Sometimes Guinan was so intuitive it was almost scary. He watched her build the drink. The food slot could have delivered it ready-made, but there was a need in the human soul to watch a recreational drink being prepared. Besides, the preparation gave both bartender and customer more time to talk, a friendly tradition that had survived for centuries on many planets.

She set the tall glass before him. Red tendrils leaked into the clear liquid from a cherry speared with a green plastic spaceship in the shape of a dart. While Wesley chewed on the cherry, Guinan said, "You never take study breaks, Wesley. You're more likely to study all night."

"Yeah, well," he said and played with the little plastic spaceship.

She continued wiping the bar.

Wesley took a deep breath and said, "I don't know if I'll make a good officer."

"Is it important that you know right now? Seems to me you have your hands full going to school and serving on the bridge."

Wesley shrugged. It was important. If he wouldn't make a good officer, a good commander, he might as well leave the *Enterprise* and Starfleet altogether. He sipped his clear ether. It was cold and sweet.

"So it's important," Guinan said. "Captain Picard has already given you more responsibility than he would entrust to the average kid your age. You seem to be doing pretty well with it."

Wesley shrugged again. "That's not command," he said. "That's just delegated authority."

"Oh," Guinan said and nodded as if she understood. Maybe she did.

"I want command. Life-and-death decisions that have to be made in a split second. I need to test myself against a starship in crisis."

"I see." She added more seltzer to Wesley's glass. He watched the fizz bubble and jump. She said, "How do cadets test themselves against starships in crisis without killing anybody?"

19

"Starfleet sets up scenarios in a holoroom at the Academy."

Guinan smiled and raised her eyebrows.

Wesley was suddenly excited. "The holodeck, of course."

Guinan nodded.

"Why didn't I think of that?"

"You were too close to the problem. You were looking for a real solution, when in this case fantasy will do just as well."

"Right, right. Do you think the holodeck has a command training program?"

"One way to find out."

He thanked Guinan and left Ten Forward without finishing his drink. The turbolift took him to deck eleven where the holodeck computer told him that various training programs and subroutines were available. Wesley made his selection and entered.

He started his training in the holodeck version of Picard's ready room and set himself problems involving real-time ship-related decisions: Should a particular crew member be promoted? What is the proper discipline for a particular infraction? What is the proper diplomatic maneuver to use when dealing with an angry or recalcitrant alien dignitary?

Wesley did not get a perfect score on any of the problems, but his rating was always in the green, or acceptable, range. According to the computer, nobody ever got a perfect score. One could approach perfection but never reach it.

Then he'd summoned up the bridge of the *Enterprise* on the holodeck, manned as it really was manned, except that he was the captain instead of Picard. He had tried his negotiating skills with Klingon renegades and Ferengi and was now testing them against Romulans. It was like playing a swift game of 3-D chess with the computer.

Wesley had studied the famous encounters with the Klingons, the Ferengi, and the Romulans. He had the same data the computer had, so the tactics of the adversaries were predictable within a certain range. It was the predictability that bothered Wesley. The Starfleet charge, "to boldly go where no one has gone before," meant that predictability would be the exception rather than the rule.

The ready room was so quiet and he was thinking so hard that the pleasant female voice of the computer made him jump when it said, "Lieutenant Shubunkin is waiting for you outside the holodeck."

"Uh-oh," Wesley said. "Stop program."

Since he was alone, the only thing that showed Wesley the computer had complied was that the spiny fish in the tank across the room seemed to freeze.

The computer said, "Do you wish this program saved?"

Wesley considered his alternatives. He had learned pretty much all he could from challenging the computer. It was fun, but it was basically a game for kids. He'd have to dig a little deeper, maybe design his own aliens. If he wanted Romulans again, he could have them. Their characteristics were in the computer's permanent memory. Wesley stood up and called out, "Cancel program and admit Lieutenant Shubunkin."

Without a sound the captain's ready room wavered

21

and disappeared, leaving Wesley at one side of a big room that was featureless but for a doorway and the grid markings on all six interior surfaces. The doors slid open, and Lieutenant Shubunkin strode in. Angrily he said, "We had an appointment."

"Yes, sir. I just lost track of the time."

"Not a healthy characteristic in an ensign," Shubunkin said. "Evidently Dr. Crusher is experiencing the same difficulty."

"What difficulty is that?"

Dr. Crusher stepped into the room. She planted her fists deep in the pockets of her smock and looked at Shubunkin with her eyebrows up, daring him to accuse her of anything at all. Wesley generally wilted when his mom looked at him that way, and evidently Dr. Crusher's hard, clear gaze had the same effect on Lieutenant Shubunkin. He said, "I am merely eager to begin."

"So begin," Dr. Crusher said and shrugged in Wesley's direction, making Wesley smile.

"Computer," Shubunkin said.

"Ready."

"Run read-only program 'Baldwin.'"

Immediately the three of them were standing in the middle of an alien jungle. Chattering, squealing, and feral noises with no earthly name came from all around. Lumps of polished wood as big as houses were caught in nets of vines that hummed as the light, spicy wind blew through them. Twirling things sailed among tangles of trees with thin trunks that rose to incredible heights. Wesley could not see the sky because of the patchwork of leaves overhead.

"Hot, isn't it?" he said as he pulled his collar away

from his neck with a finger. He, Dr. Crusher, and Lieutenant Shubunkin sat down on crystalline rocks that thrust from among the dead brown leaves like giants' teeth.

The only things that spoiled the perfect illusion were the standard English words floating in midair and the dramatic music. The words said, "Omniology presents 'The Alien Universe of Eric Baldwin.'"

Baldwin was an exologist, an expert on alien cultures and their artifacts. He was a tall wiry man with the face of a benign demon. According to the documentary, he had escaped death many times, usually either just before or just after making an important discovery. An entire wing of the North American Museum of Extraterrestrial Biology was named after him.

As the program continued, the crystal rocks they were sitting on became toadstools, rock outcroppings, coral reefs, and finally, merely chairs. Along the way Baldwin was threatened by angry natives, kidnapped by pirates and smugglers of both the water and space variety, twisted through weird dimensions by alien artifacts, and pursued by rival exologists. Each time he was threatened with death or worse, he managed to narrowly escape, using an impressive combination of creativity and physical strength. The documentary ended, leaving Dr. Crusher, Wesley, and Shubunkin standing on the blank holodeck. Dr. Crusher said, "A very impressive career."

"Captain Picard says he's the single most important exologist in the Federation."

"The captain should know," Dr. Crusher said. "They went to school together."

Shubunkin said, "Perhaps. But there are other exologists . . ."

He allowed the observation to dangle, but neither Wesley nor Dr. Crusher took hold of it. Personally, Wesley suspected that Lieutenant Shubunkin was just jealous. Dr. Crusher only said, "You may be right," thanked him for running the documentary, and went back to sickbay, still visibly pining for Eric Baldwin.

After the door had knitted itself shut with a pneumatic sigh, Lieutenant Shubunkin and Ensign Crusher watched it as if they thought it might open again. Shubunkin said, "On my planet, if someone says 'You may be right,' that is what they mean. I think your mother means something else."

"You may be right," Wesley said, and immediately wished he hadn't. He went on quickly, "I'd like to ask you a question."

"Proceed."

Wesley took a deep breath and said, "I want to design some aliens I can practice my diplomatic skills on." Wesley didn't want to admit his self-doubts about his command abilities. Not to Shubunkin, anyway.

Shubunkin said, "By aliens, I assume you mean nonhumans."

"Of course."

Wesley could see why most of the bridge crew had difficulty getting along with Shubunkin. Even Counselor Troi, who could get along with anybody, found him a little abrasive. The guy knew his stuff, but he was too ready to show it off. Wesley took a deep breath and said, "Yes, sir. I mean nonhumans."

"The *Enterprise* computers hold a detailed description of every encounter between races since the founding of the Federation. Surely by using those descriptions, the computer can design something that will satisfy you."

"Actually, sir, I was looking for something a little more unusual."

Shubunkin nodded and said, "You want more interesting aliens. Faster, less predictable aliens."

"Right. Absolutely."

Shubunkin stroked his chin. He said, "The Borders scale might be of use."

"Borders scale?"

"It's a complex scale of social, intellectual, and emotional values. Among other things, six different kinds of creativity are listed, as well as honor, courage, mercy, fierceness, ruthlessness, arrogance, and mental and physical speed. Hundreds of categories. I believe Borders even created a subsection concerning sense of humor. Her scale is a useful tool when trying to quantify similarities and differences between races."

Wesley squinted as he considered the possibilities. He said, "There must be more to it than just plugging in random numbers."

"Certainly. The first value to some extent defines what the second must be. The first and second together help define the third. All creatures are consistent within their own system. The thing that makes one race seem alien to another is the difference between their systems."

Wesley saw that creating a new alien, even using the

Borders scale, would be quite a challenge. After learning all he could about the scale from the library computer, he could probably get Geordi La Forge to help with the programming.

The computer said, "Personal memo for Wesley Crusher: Your bridge watch begins in ten minutes."

"Acknowledged. Thanks, Lieutenant. You've been a big help."

"I'm sure."

As Wesley walked quickly from the room, he wondered if Shubunkin was being arrogant again or if this was another case of his saying what he meant. Wesley could not help feeling that Shubunkin was strange, even for a first-contact specialist.

As the *Enterprise* dropped out of warp, Picard glanced at the man in the seat on his right. He was large and round with side-whiskers rather longer than regulations allowed. His thick face shone as if he were sweating despite the controlled climate of the *Enterprise*. His chubby fingers never stopped moving on the arms of the chair. The form-fitting design of the Starfleet uniform did not make him look thinner, though the short cape he affected helped. Commander Riker stood behind and above him, next to Worf at the tactical rail.

Ensign Crusher came onto the bridge with a minute to spare before his watch began. Winston-Smyth gave up her chair at the conn, and Wesley sat down, immediately logging in his arrival with a few deft touches on the control panel.

Feeling much too much like a tour guide, Picard said, "We've just dropped out of warp, Commander

Mont. Mr. Data, how long till we reach Tantamon Four?"

"Fourteen minutes and twenty-two seconds, sir."

"Let's have it on screen."

On the main viewscreen, the forward star field wavered and an Earth-type planet appeared. From this distance, Tantamon IV seemed to be covered with gray-green moss on which some cotton wool had snagged. Picard was always amazed how many planets looked like that from space, like the human home world. The *Enterprise* was his home, but like many humans, Picard felt a spiritual connection to the green hills of Terra that never quite went away.

"Standard orbit, Mr. Crusher."

"Aye, sir."

Commander Mont smiled, and his hands were still. He looked like a hungry man mesmerized by a table laden with food, Picard thought.

In his gruff voice, Mont said, "It's a likely-looking place."

Likely for what? Picard wondered. Mont seemed to enjoy saying things that barely made sense. Still, he was the one Starfleet had sent to debrief Baldwin after his six months on the planet below. Mont must be good at his job.

The aft turbolift doors opened, and Lieutenant Shubunkin entered the bridge. With his eyes on the screen, he stepped forward.

Picard said, "Mr. Worf, please inform Professor Baldwin of our imminent arrival."

"Aye, sir."

Tantamon IV turned placidly below them for a few seconds. Worf said, "I have Professor Baldwin."

"On screen," said Riker.

The picture on the viewscreen was replaced by a steamy planetary scene. Baldwin, ever the showman as well as the scientist, stood in such a way that Picard and the others on the bridge could see a silver teardrop shape lying in the humid alien jungle behind him. Next to him stood an alien. Based on what Picard had seen in preliminary reports, he assumed it was one of the Tantamon natives.

The jungle was recognizable as such, steamy and dense, but unlike the wild earthly jungle growth that was mostly vertical, the Tantamon jungle seemed to be mostly horizontal, made entirely of bowls of various sizes, shapes, and colors. Buggy eyes looked over the rims from inside some of the larger ones. Above each buggy eye was a bright blue cranium.

The alien standing next to Baldwin was probably typical of his race. He—if human sexes meant anything—was on the edge of being human. He had tiny bowls for ears and a shiny blue exoskeleton, which gave him a faintly insectoid appearance. Adding to this were the things at the ends of his arms, not hands but delicate pincers with gripping grooves in them. He might have been wearing clothing. Picard could not tell.

Baldwin had grown a beard since Picard had seen him last. Sweat darkened his shirt under his arms and on his chest. His hair was a little wild, and more sweat dripped from strings of it that drooped across his forehead. He looked dashing and wonderful, as he did on the Omniology holochips in *Enterprise*'s library. Picard, not going in much for vanity, had no idea how dashing and wonderful he himself looked to many people and so felt a small pang of jealousy, which he quickly suppressed.

"It's beautiful," Mont said.

Picard knew that Mont wasn't talking about Baldwin or the alien or even the jungle, though the jungle was certainly beautiful, once one dumped one's earthly prejudices about what a jungle should look like. Mont was talking about the silver teardrop. All sensor readings that Baldwin had taken matched up nicely with the sensor readings the *Enterprise* had taken months before in the Omega Triangulae region. The teardrop was beautiful scientifically as well as aesthetically.

"Good to see you, Jean-Luc," said Baldwin.

"And you, old friend. Do you need help packing?"

"No, thanks. I travel pretty light." He smiled.

Picard said, "So I remember. Prepare to beam up."

"Right, Jean-Luc. See you soon."

As he turned away, the screen once more showed the mossy ball of Tantamon IV.

"What do you think of that, then, eh, Shubunkin?" Mont said.

"I think that I do not yet have enough to think about."

"Right you are." Mont rose to his feet with surprising grace and moved like a thundercloud to the aft turbolift. "Come along, Shubunkin. We will meet and greet Professor Baldwin."

The two of them got into the turbolift, and the doors closed. Counselor Troi began to speak, but Picard put up a hand to silence her. He knew the turbolift doors would open again in a moment, and they did. Lieutenant Shubunkin stepped out and said, "Which transporter room?"

"Number three," said Picard, trying not to smile. "Deck six."

Shubunkin nodded and ducked back into the turbolift.

"Now, Counselor, what is it?"

"There is something odd about Commander Mont."

"And his playmate, Shubunkin, too," Riker said.

"That is not what I mean," Troi went on. "Lieutenant Shubunkin is merely a little formal and much too impressed with himself. But I've thought all along that Commander Mont is hiding something. I would not trust him."

"He's a Starfleet officer," Riker said.

"Even Starfleet officers have secrets."

"Logged and noted, Counselor. Mr. Data, make our guest comfortable." As Data stood up and walked toward the turbolift doors, Picard looked at them as if seeing through them and said, "And see if you can be of any use to Commander Mont."

"Understood, Captain," Data said as the doors closed.

Chapter Two

BEFORE DISAPPEARING into his ready room, the captain ordered Wesley to head for Memory Alpha at warp five. At that velocity they would be traveling for two weeks. They could have safely traveled much faster, but Commander Mont and Lieutenant Shubunkin needed time to debrief Baldwin and get a first approximation of his findings on Tantamon IV. Later Baldwin would spend months, maybe years, at Memory Alpha, studying and organizing his data until he'd drawn from it all the conclusions he could. Other scholars would come later, building their work on his.

For the moment, however, Starfleet was very eager to learn anything they could about the aliens in the silver teardrop. Were they friend or foe? What could the Federation and these new aliens learn from each other?

The hours of Wesley's watch dragged by. Memory Alpha, the central information depository of the

Federation, was a well-known destination. There was nothing between them and it but empty space. No Romulans, no Ferengi, no Borg. Nothing but the unexpected, and one, Wesley thought, could get a little too clever about always expecting it. If necessary, the *Enterprise* could fly itself to Memory Alpha. Wesley's presence at the conn was almost a formality.

Captain Picard was in his ready room, and Counselor Troi was off on some errand of mercy. Commander Riker was on the bridge and would be available in an emergency if one should arise, but at the moment he was grunting over the composition of one of the many reports Starfleet inevitably required.

Data was where Wesley wanted to be, with Professor Eric Baldwin. Wesley shook his head in wonderment. What a guy that Baldwin was. Wesley wondered what kind of a smart, arrogant, warlike imaginary alien Baldwin could come up with, Borders scale or no.

Wesley knew many of the women on the ship were having lusty fantasies about Baldwin. Never before had Wesley thought of sweat as sexy, but there it was. He wondered if he would ever understand women. The fact that even Riker was occasionally mystified by them did not give him hope.

When his watch was over Wesley went to his cabin, keyed into the ship's library computer, and looked up the Borders scale. To his chagrin, he discovered that it was less a shopping list than an encyclopedia of characteristics. The instructions alone—page after page of cultural jargon and mathematical formulas— took up three volumes.

Wesley sighed and dived in. He became fascinated.

But when he came up for air some hours later, he found that he had barely begun. He didn't mind working hard for what he learned—finding a subject that could make him sweat was a pleasant change—but he was in a hurry. He wanted to invent those challenging aliens right now. He thought about giving one of the characteristics a number at random, just to get the ball rolling. But that was too much like cheating, and cheating, even if it seemed necessary, never appealed to him.

He drummed his fingers on the table while he considered what to do next. The answer was obvious. When he had a computer problem, there was only one person for him to go to.

Wesley found Data in his cabin harassing his own computer terminal. When Wesley entered, Data looked up, his fingers poised over the keyboard, his face holding its usual expression of mild surprise.

"What are you working on?" Wesley said.

"Some research for the captain," Data said and blanked the screen.

"Does it have to do with Commander Mont?"

"That would be a logical assumption," Data said, admitting nothing. "Was there something you wanted to discuss?"

"Yeah. Do you know anything about the Borders scale?"

"It is a quantitative scale of the physical, emotional, and rational characteristics of various races. It is used—theoretically—to compare them in an unbiased and logical way."

"Theoretically?"

"Of course. As you must know, any such scale

reflects the biases of its creator, in this case of Dr. Sandra Borders, senior exobiology librarian at Memory Alpha."

"So it's no good at all, then," Wesley said glumly. He'd have to look elsewhere for a solution to his alien problem.

"Some researchers take the scale very seriously. But Vulcans, despite their penchant for logic, dislike the system because of its built-in prejudices. Others take the romantic, and perhaps more correct, view that any such catalog is bound to be incomplete and therefore is no better than a distant approximation."

"What do *you* think of it?"

Data cocked his head. From long experience, Wesley knew this meant he was about to fling a zinger of a question. Data said, "I think it can be useful if used with the proper care. Why do you ask?"

Data was his friend. He could trust Data with his innermost hopes and fears. Wesley said, "I'm testing my ability to command by using Starfleet training programs."

"Ah. And how will the Borders scale help?"

"I want to design an alien that will challenge me, that will help me find out if I'll ever be good enough to be captain of a starship."

"No such alien exists."

"Right."

"Ah. Then you wish to create such an alien and interact with it."

"Right."

Data leaned back in his chair and picked up a calabash pipe that lay in a nearby ashtray. Affecting the mannerisms of Sherlock Holmes, he tapped the stem of the pipe against his teeth, something he did occasionally when considering a problem. Wesley had never seen him actually light the pipe, but just holding it made Data seem more thoughtful.

Data sprang to his feet and began to pace the cabin. He had plenty of room. Data had fewer personal possessions than anyone else Wesley knew. In a clipped Holmesian accent, he said, "You wish to design an alien of superior cunning and intelligence, yet entirely without compassion."

"Right," Wesley said again. "Just for the holodeck."

"Of course." Data sat down, laid the pipe carefully in the ashtray, and began typing into the computer terminal. His hands moved very fast, were almost a blur. Wesley stood behind him, watching. In a few seconds, Data reviewed what had taken Wesley hours to read. Then Data leapt into unfamiliar territory.

Scarcely ten minutes later Data stopped. He popped a clear cylindrical chip into the slot on the terminal, touched a few keys, and seconds later handed the chip to Wesley. It was now a pale blue. "This chip contains the parameters of the aliens you desire along with the Borders scale equations. I suggest you ask Lieutenant Commander La Forge to help you install them in the holodeck computer. No one knows more about the *Enterprise* systems than he does."

"Thanks, Data." Wesley bounced the chip in one hand while he looked over Data's shoulder at the schematic of the *Enterprise* on the wall.

"Was there something else, Wesley?"

Wesley smiled at his own presumption. He never

thought of himself as a fan type. He said, "Tell me. What is Professor Baldwin really like?"

"Like? He is a white human male, almost two meters tall and weighing slightly more than one hundred kilograms."

Wesley smiled as he shook his head. Evidently Data had even less inclination to be a fan than he did.

"Is that funny?" Data said.

"Usually when people ask what someone is like, they want to know about the individual's personality and whether they have pleasing features."

A little confused, Data said, "He seemed pleasant enough."

"Okay, Data. Thanks."

Wesley left the cabin as quickly as seemed polite. He didn't want to spend the rest of the day discussing human attractiveness with an android.

Captain Picard sat at one end of the big obsidian slab that served as a table in the conference lounge just off the bridge. He tried not to stare while he wondered again what it was in Commander Mont that Starfleet found valuable. Mont had a certain blustery charm, but he seemed to know no more about aliens than Lieutenant Shubunkin did. There were times when Picard was convinced that Mont knew considerably less.

For instance, when Mont and Shubunkin had first come on board at Starbase 123, Picard had thrown a small formal dinner to welcome them. During the dinner, talk had turned to the hot exobiology topic of the moment—a newly discovered race, the Trilg. They were unusual in that while they had grasping organs very much like human hands, they had no technology whatsoever. Not so much as a rock with which to kill one of the local herbivores for food. Not so much as a cave in which to live. Starfleet specialists with high extrasensory ratings could detect no evidence of unusual mental activity. Were the Trilg intelligent or were they not? And if they were not, why not?

Lieutenant Shubunkin had gone on at length, spinning a gossamer theory supported by obscure ideas about racial talent, harmful solar rays, and synchronistic curves. The ideas were no more than theories themselves. Picard had thought all his arguments pretty unlikely, and Riker had politely argued with Shubunkin; but beyond making a few off-color comments, Commander Mont had said nothing. Picard was certain that before Shubunkin began to speak, Mont had not even heard of the Trilg.

This was an expert on first contact?

The next morning Picard had asked Troi what her impression of Mont was.

"He seems to be very satisfied with himself."

"Not shy?" Picard asked.

"I detected no unease last night. However . . ." She looked to one side, pursed her lips, and shook her head. When she looked at the captain again, it was with the direct, guileless stare Picard had come to trust. Troi said, "He is definitely hiding something. There is a tension in him, a waiting."

"For what?"

"I have no idea."

Picard had asked her to tell him more if anything occurred to her, but so far, except for making a similar observation on the bridge a few hours earlier, Troi had said nothing about Commander Mont.

Troi was next to the captain now, staring out the port at the rainbow smudges that the warp field made of the stars. At the other end of the table, Mont and Shubunkin were having a quiet conversation.

Despite the evidence of his own observations and instincts, despite the corroborative feelings of Counselor Troi, Data's research into Commander Mont's background had turned up nothing unusual. He'd gone to school, he'd come up through the ranks in a very normal way, he'd published the following papers. The man was a puzzle, and Picard did not like it.

The door sighed open, and Mr. Data entered with Professor Baldwin. Baldwin had showered and changed into a clean bush outfit. It was khaki, neatly pressed, and sporting many pockets, just the way it had come from the clothing fabricator. He had trimmed his beard, but it was still there, giving his face a faintly demonic look that, Picard understood, women found attractive.

Picard and Baldwin shook hands and clasped each other's shoulders, made social noises about how long it had been, and indeed, they had not seen each other for at least fifteen years. While Data sat down on the captain's other side, Baldwin shook hands all around, lingering a little over Troi's. Troi did not seem to mind.

"Welcome aboard the *Enterprise,*" Picard said.

"Thank you, Captain."

"Settling in all right?"

Baldwin sat down and said, "Yes, fine. I understand it's two weeks to Memory Alpha."

"At warp five, yes," Picard said.

Baldwin frowned, but Mont said, "Barely enough time to begin."

Shubunkin said, "We can begin now. I understand there is an infowafer . . ." He held out his hand.

From one of his shirt pockets Baldwin took a green plastic square no bigger than the square of insulating tile that had come from the twentieth-century space shuttle *Enterprise* and was now in stasis in one of the rec rooms.

As Baldwin handed the infowafer to Shubunkin, Data said, "It is only a copy. The original is in the safe in Lieutenant Worf's office."

"Just as well," Shubunkin said. "Six months' worth of data."

"Including," Baldwin said as he raised one finger, "the entire contents of the alien ship's computer memory."

"You were able to download it?" Shubunkin said, obviously surprised.

"All part of the job."

Troi's shy, self-deprecating smile matched Baldwin's.

"Gentlemen," said Picard, "you have your work cut out for you, and a limited time in which to do it. Please proceed."

Mont and Shubunkin stood up and, as one, made a short bow toward Picard's end of the table. The door sighed open, and they stood there looking back at Baldwin. "Coming, Professor?" Shubunkin said.

"In a minute. I want to talk to Jean-Luc, er, the captain."

"We will be in the exobiology lab on deck five."

"I'll be there," Baldwin said, a little too brightly.

When the door closed behind Mont and Shubunkin, Baldwin opened his arms and smiled apologetically. Counselor Troi stood up and held out her hand for Baldwin to shake again. She said, "Come on, Data."

"Captain?" Data said.

"I believe Professor Baldwin wishes a private conference."

Looking a little confused, Data said, "Aye, Captain," and left with Counselor Troi.

When they were gone, Baldwin walked to the food dispenser and said, "A Randy Yeoman." He looked at Picard, who nodded. "Make that two," Baldwin said. A moment later two tall, sweating glasses with red smoke in them appeared on the stage of the dispenser. Baldwin picked up both of them, gave one to Picard, then sat down in the seat Data had just vacated.

They toasted old times, and then Baldwin said, "Command agrees with you, Jean-Luc."

"As it never did with you. But you landed on your feet as you always have. Fame. Fortune. Adventure. You have the life you always said you wanted."

"Yes. And the enemies to go with it."

Baldwin took a long drink while Picard said, "Oh?"

"This is good," Baldwin said as he peered into his drink. "I tried to make an alcoholic beverage from some of the plants on Tantamon Four. Couldn't do it. Something wrong with their sugars or something. I never figured it out."

"You were busy with the alien ship. What about those enemies?"

"I've been an exologist for a long time. I've rubbed a lot of faces in the dirt, even without trying."

Picard waited.

"Do you know how many people hate me for getting someplace first, for finding something first, for drawing correct conclusions first, for sending artifacts and information to Starfleet and Federation museums rather than selling them to the highest bidder?"

"How many?"

"A lot," said Baldwin and set his drink loudly onto the table.

When he did not speak for a few moments, Picard said, "So you want out."

"You bet I do. I want to die in bed, not in some forsaken backwater where I was sent by a museum." He took another drink and said, "Two weeks is a long time."

Picard smiled. "Surely you can't feel yourself in danger aboard the *Enterprise.*"

"Silly, huh? Paranoia will get me if nothing else does. Pretty soon I'll be balling up antique newspapers and scattering them around my bed so that nobody can sneak up on me while I'm sleeping." He shook his head.

"You must have a plan."

"Yes. There is always a plan. I'm going to disappear."

"That will be difficult on Memory Alpha."

"Ships stop at Memory Alpha. And they leave again."

They studied each other for a while. Picard could sympathize with Baldwin. There had been moments

—when life-and-death decisions had to be made, when confronting situations from which there seemed to be no escape—when he had considered disappearing himself. He understood from Troi that people in responsible positions frequently had such fantasies. But fantasies were all they were, and Picard knew it. He could captain a freighter or a cruise ship. He could become a farmer on some frontier world. He could even teach at the Academy. Certainly, and be bored in a week.

Quietly Picard said, "Risk is in your blood as it is in mine. The risk takes different forms, but it is there just as certainly."

"Not anymore, Jean-Luc."

Picard finished his drink and said, "If all you want is an ear, I'm certain Counselor Troi would be glad to oblige."

"An ear is only the beginning. I want your help."

"If I don't deposit you at Memory Alpha, people are sure to notice."

"You'll think of something." Baldwin stood up and went on, "You're the captain." He left the conference lounge.

Picard watched the rainbow smudges go by, while wondering if he really would think of something. And if he did, would he tell Baldwin?

Wesley found Lieutenant Commander Geordi La Forge in Engineering sitting at a table almost as large as the one in the conference lounge. Set into the top was a variety of gauges, readouts, telltales, and controls. This was the master situation monitor, and from here, anyone who knew how could follow the flow and flux of energy and information throughout the entire ship.

La Forge looked up at Wesley. At least he turned his head in Wesley's direction. He pointed to a screen on which a sine curve was having fits. "Warp efficiency is down three percent, and I don't know why."

Wesley had been astonished by La Forge when they first met. La Forge had been born blind, and in order to see wore a piece of hardware called a VISOR, a mobile sensing rig that covered his eyes and hooked directly into his nervous system at cyborg ports just in front of his ears. Wesley had needed some time to get used to the VISOR, and La Forge had joked that, like the floating wooden eyeball Mark Twain had spoken of, "it made the children cry." To Wesley's knowledge, the VISOR had never made anyone cry, though whether La Forge actually could *see* was still a matter of debate among medical experts.

"I get around without bumping into stuff," La Forge had said, "and that's enough for me."

Wesley looked over La Forge's shoulder at the screen and said, "Three percent is within specs, isn't it?"

"Sure it is. Better than specs. But that doesn't mean I don't want to know why." He touched a lighted square on the table, and the sine wave smoothed out. "What can I do for you, Wesley?"

"I'm having sort of a problem with the holodeck."

"Nothing maintenance can take care of, I trust?"

"Uh, no." Wesley showed him the pale blue cylinder and said, "Data gave me this. It's a program that uses the Borders scale to define an artificial alien. Can you help me install it in the holodeck computer?"

La Forge took the chip and stood it up on the table. He leaned back in his chair, laced his fingers over his flat belly, and said, "What's all this about, Wes?"

Wesley looked around. The engineering staff was busy taking readings and doing general maintenance. They weren't close enough to hear even if they were listening. Wesley took a deep breath and told La Forge about his problem.

When Wesley was done, La Forge shook his head and said, "Wes, you remind me of a kid I know back home. Ryan is four years old and scared to death of Starfleet Academy."

Wesley could see a parable coming, but he couldn't resist asking, "Why?"

"He's desperate to go into space, see. But he's afraid that when it's time for him to enter Starfleet Academy he'll still be four years old. He won't understand anything, and he'll only come up to the other cadets' knees."

"Too soon to worry, huh?" Wesley said. He sat down across the table from La Forge and rested a cheek on his fist.

"That's what I think. By the time they give you a starship to command, you'll be ready. Starfleet doesn't give out Galaxy-class starships like lollipops, you know."

Wesley watched the gently bobbing life-support indicators. La Forge was wrong. Wesley didn't know how to explain how important it was to know *right now* if he had any aptitude for command. Important decisions had to be made about his life. Who wanted to wait till they were old before they found out if they were any good at a job they'd wanted all their life?

La Forge said, "What do you call this program of yours, Wes?"

Wesley shrugged and said, "Boogeymen."

La Forge smiled, and Wesley could not help smiling back.

The alarm Klaxon went off, and the calm computer voice said, "Intruder alert. Intruder alert. Please secure your area. Please secure your area. This is not a drill. Intru—" The computer voice was cut off.

"What the hell?" said La Forge.

"What the hell?" said Captain Picard when he saw Professor Baldwin's cabin. In front of him Lieutenant Worf only growled.

Chapter Three

COMMANDER MONT lay on the deck with blood several shades lighter than human blood leaking out of him. There was quite a puddle already. Standing over him, still breathing hard, was Professor Baldwin. His new bush shirt was torn and his hair was mussed. He tossed the dagger he was holding to Picard. Picard caught it—by the hilt, thank goodness—and inspected it. The dagger was oddly shaped, covered with gems, and very sharp. He handed it to Worf, who said, "Axerii."

"Mont doesn't look Axerii," Picard said.

Dr. Crusher pushed past Picard and Worf and knelt next to Mont. She touched him here and there and aimed a medical tricorder at him, but even from where he was standing, Picard could tell he was dead.

"He's dead, Captain."

"Yes, yes. Would you care to explain what happened here, Professor?"

Professor Baldwin collapsed into a chair and let his hands dangle between his knees. While looking at the floor he said, "Shubunkin and Mont and I finished our first session a while ago. I was a little surprised when Mont came to my door, but he said he needed something cleared up right away. I let him in."

"Imprudent," said Worf.

"Yeah. As it turned out." He looked up. "The guy pulled a dagger on me. That Axerii dagger. Mont was in better shape than he looked, but while he was chasing me around the cabin I managed to sound the intruder alert. After he was dead it didn't seem relevant anymore, so I canceled it."

Troi had been correct. Mont had been hiding something, and apparently that thing was his ambition to murder Professor Baldwin.

Still kneeling, Dr. Crusher said, "Mont isn't human, Captain. His readings are Axerii."

"Just like the dagger," Worf said.

Crusher gently pulled away the bloody Starfleet uniform. Underneath, wherever they wouldn't show, were fine yellow feathers, now a sloppy mess. She said, "We'll probably find that his ears are artificial. Axerii don't have any, just ear holes."

Picard said, "Can you explain Mont's actions, Professor?"

Baldwin narrowed his eyes and glared at Picard. Picard stood up to the gaze, but remembered that only a few hours earlier Baldwin had told him he wanted to disappear because he had a lot of enemies. Picard had thought Baldwin was exaggerating. Perhaps Picard had been wrong. Baldwin's look softened, and he grinned as he shook his head.

Picard touched his insignia and said, "Number One?"

"Here, Captain."

"Commander Mont was apparently an Axerii assassin sent to murder Professor Baldwin. Inform Starfleet. If one mole has burrowed into the organization, there are sure to be others. And please extend my compliments to Counselor Troi. She was right about Mont."

There was a moment of silence. Picard imagined his first officer glancing around, taking in the new data, and nodding. "Aye, Captain."

"Mr. Worf, please inform Lieutenant Shubunkin that I would like to see him in my ready room."

"Aye, Captain."

"Come along, Professor."

Professor Baldwin followed Picard along the corridors of the *Enterprise* to the turbolift. The doors closed, Picard said, "Bridge," and the turbolift began to move. After listening to the whine of the machinery for a moment, he glanced at Baldwin and saw a little boy trying his best to appear contrite for having been caught with a handful of cookies. The performance was charming, but Picard was unwilling to be convinced. He felt his jaw tighten, and he took a deep breath to loosen it. He said, "You will have to make a full report eventually, Eric, but I confess that I am curious right now. What did you do to make the Axerii so angry?"

"You don't want to know."

"Don't play that game with me, Eric," Picard commanded. "I know it too well."

"Yeah." Baldwin frowned and said, "The Axerii and I were after the same thing: the mating ritual of the Yahk Shimash."

"I thought the Yahk Shimash were extinct."

The turbolift doors opened onto the main bridge. Picard stepped out and motioned Baldwin to follow. As he walked down the ramp to his ready room, Picard said, "Everything under control, Number One?"

"Yes, sir."

"I'll be expecting some visitors. Please hurry them along."

"Yes, sir."

In the ready room Picard requested two cups of hot Earl Grey tea from the food slot, gave one to Baldwin, and sat down behind his desk with the other. "You were saying?" said Picard.

Baldwin sipped his tea and said, "We thought the Yahk Shimash were extinct, too. But after I'd been on Shim for almost an entire local year, I found what must have been the last existing tribe. I spent a lot of time with them and found out what I wanted to know."

"Then the Axerii arrived."

"Bingo. They arrived and began spoiling everything by making enemies where I had made friends."

"That sounds like the Axerii."

"Yeah. So I talked them up until the Yahk Shimash were eager to give the Axerii a demonstration of the mating ritual, the least disgusting part of which is being buried up to the chin in a specially prepared dunghill."

Picard tried hard not to smile and failed.

Baldwin said, "The Axerii were not as amused as you are. But by the time they were married to one of the Yahk Shimash male-oids, I was gone." He scratched behind his ear and said, "I'd heard they were after me. You have any sugar for this tea?"

"Try the food dispenser." As Baldwin got up and asked the dispenser to produce some sugar, Picard said, "You don't seem nearly as worried about your real enemies as you did about the potential enemies you spoke of this afternoon."

Baldwin took a pinch of sugar from the bowl that appeared and said, "Those were just make-believe enemies. Being afraid of them is like being afraid of the bad guys in a holo. Almost entertainment, like. But"—he sat in his chair, sipped his tea, and smiled—"the Axerii are real. If I worried about them and others like them I'd be worrying all the time and going crazy because I haven't disappeared yet."

Picard was about to ask him if he still thought it necessary to disappear when the door chime twittered and instead Picard said, "Come."

Worf entered with Lieutenant Shubunkin, who stepped forward and said, "Am I under arrest, Captain?"

Picard glanced at Worf, who stiffened. People who didn't know him sometimes mistook Worf's forceful personality for belligerence. While he was not the pussycat Tasha Yar had sometimes made him out to be, he was also not the undisciplined beast that others feared.

Trying to keep a straight face for Worf's sake,

Picard said, "I'm sorry if Lieutenant Worf gave you that impression. I assure you he was escorting you for your own protection."

"Why would I need protection?"

Baldwin said, "Commander Mont is dead."

For the first time Picard saw Shubunkin's face go white. He asked what happened, and Picard explained, with the inevitable footnotes from Baldwin.

Shubunkin said, "It seems that Professor Baldwin is the one who needs the protection."

"Don't you have any enemies, Shubunkin?" Baldwin said.

"Of course. But they are academic enemies. Their weapon of choice is the scholarly paper, not the dagger."

"Let us hope you are correct," Picard said. "Working alone, Lieutenant, will you still be able to give Starfleet a preliminary report in two weeks?"

"Of course. Professor Baldwin's report on the d'Ort'd is quite complete and well organized."

"D'Ort'd?" Picard asked.

Baldwin set down his teacup and said, "That's as close as I can get to what the silver teardrop people call themselves. It probably means 'the people' or something like that. Most racial names mean that." As Baldwin got more excited, he began to outline big mountains with his hands. "As far as I can tell, the d'Ort'd take an entirely different approach to technology from the one taken by any members of the Federation. They speak of their machines the same way they speak of their bodies. I don't get it yet, but I will."

"We will," Shubunkin said.

"In two weeks?" Baldwin said and laughed.

Picard said, "Despite your assurances, Lieutenant Shubunkin, you and Professor Baldwin will both be covered by round-the-clock security, starting now." He nodded at Worf, who nodded back.

"Two weeks," Baldwin said again and shook his head.

Shubunkin attempted to look unassailable.

That evening at dinner, Wesley went over the day in his mind. It had been a *great* day. He'd learned about the Borders scale from Lieutenant Shubunkin, Data had helped him write the Boogeyman program, and Geordi had guided him through the installation process. Wesley could almost feel the Boogeymen lying in wait inside the holodeck computer. He chuckled evilly.

"What's that?" Dr. Crusher said.

"Nothing, Mom," said Wesley, embarrassed.

"You're very quiet. Except for the melodramatic grunting."

"Sorry. I was just thinking."

"You're always just thinking. About what in particular this time?"

"It's kind of personal."

"I'm your mother."

Dr. Crusher looked at him over her salad with such intensity that Wesley had to smile. She was his mother and a good doctor, but no commander. Would she understand his preoccupation with leadership ability? Hoping for the best, he said, "I've been using some

Starfleet training programs on the holodeck," and went on from there. It seemed pointless to hide anything from her anyway. As a mom, Beverly Crusher could sometimes sense things that escaped even Counselor Troi.

Wesley was pleased to see how seriously his mother took his problems. When Wesley finished, she nodded, her lips pursed, a faraway look in her eyes. She said, "I'll bet you'd learn a lot more if somebody was there when you made a mistake."

"I've studied the books. You can't get the stuff I want to learn out of books."

"Not a book mistake. An experience mistake." Dr. Crusher became excited by her own idea. "I'll bet Captain Picard would join you on the holodeck."

"The captain's awfully busy," Wesley said, visions of Picard's disapproving expression dancing in his head.

"Nonsense," Dr. Crusher said. "A robot freighter could do the run between here and Memory Alpha."

"I don't think this is a good idea."

"You don't want me to speak with him?"

This entire line of discussion made Wesley very nervous. He knew the captain was not comfortable around children, and for all that the captain had made him a real ensign instead of just an acting one, Wesley knew that Picard still considered him a child. A large child. A smart and dependable child. But a child nonetheless. Wesley said, "Talk to him if you want to. Just don't tell him it was my idea."

"Of course not," Dr. Crusher said. "I want the credit."

For the rest of the meal, Wesley managed to direct the conversation away from his activities on the holodeck.

The next day as Wesley's watch on the bridge came to an end, the captain appeared at the ready room door and beckoned him inside. When the captain was settled behind his desk, he said, "Dr. Crusher tells me that you've been running the Starfleet training programs on the holodeck."

Wesley suddenly felt icy. There were no regulations against what he was doing. He'd checked. Still, he might have missed something. "Yes, sir."

"Have you run the *Kobayashi Maru* scenario?"

"No, sir." Wesley had never heard of it.

"It's quite a pretty problem, really. Starfleet used to run it with the Klingons. The most recent versions use Romulans or Ferengi, sometimes both together. Shall we give it a try?" Picard seemed enthusiastic, as if this would be as big an adventure for him as for Wesley.

"Sure. I mean, yes, sir." Somehow they had gone from an abstract discussion of Wesley's use of the holodeck to the very practical consideration of whether Captain Picard would join him. How did you say no to the captain? Did Wesley even want to try?

Wesley followed Captain Picard through the bridge and into the turbolift. Data slid in with them just before the doors closed.

"Just coming off watch, Mr. Data?" Picard said.

Wesley suddenly knew what was coming. Why not? he thought. Why not invite the whole damn bridge crew?

"Yes, sir," said Data.

"If you have nothing special planned, perhaps you would care to join Ensign Crusher and me on the holodeck. We're going to run the *Kobayashi Maru* scenario." Picard actually sounded as if he was looking forward to observing Wesley's performance. But maybe he wasn't just interested in Wesley. Maybe the captain was reliving his time at the Academy.

"Indeed I would, sir. I would like very much to see Ensign Crusher's new aliens in action."

"New aliens?" asked the captain.

Wesley said, "Yes, sir. Boogeymen. Lieutenant Shubunkin, Data, and Lieutenant Commander La Forge helped me work them out."

"Using the Borders scale, no doubt."

"Yes, sir," Data said.

Wesley shook his head. Had everybody heard of the Borders scale but him?

Picard looked around, realized they weren't moving, and said, "Deck eleven."

Wesley brought up the bridge of the *Enterprise* on the holodeck, asked for the *Kobayashi Maru* training scenario with the Boogeyman modifications. Wesley was a little nervous about taking the center seat with the captain there, but Picard insisted. "No point in doing this at all if I act as captain," he said. He took the conn while Data sat at Ops. On the main screen a normal-looking star field came toward them at warp speed.

Wesley tried to get comfortable in the command chair. He didn't know what the *Kobayashi Maru* was, but it didn't seem so bad so far.

Picard leaned toward Data and said, "You know, in

the old days, Starfleet actually had to build mock starship bridges in order to run their training scenarios."

"Interesting," said Data. With sudden seriousness, he said, "Transmission coming in."

"On audio," Wesley said.

Picard smiled at him and turned to his control board.

A broken signal came in. Most of it was garbled or obscured by static. "Mayday, Mayday," it said. "This is the freighter, *Kobayashi Maru*. All systems failing. Help desperately needed. Any ship within hailing distance, please help."

"Location of *Kobayashi Maru*?" Wesley said.

Data scanned his board and said, "One two three seven mark four. The Romulan Neutral Zone."

"Oops," said Wesley, a little too loudly. Picard glanced at him appraisingly. "Uh," said Wesley, "tactical."

The freighter's distress message continued to come in while Wesley studied the display now on the main screen. *Enterprise* was the blue flashing light on the Federation side of the Neutral Zone. Just the other side of the open fence that represented the Neutral Zone, the *Kobayashi Maru* was represented by an amber pulse. No Romulan vessels were on the screen, but they wouldn't show up if they were cloaked.

"Data?" Wesley said.

"It could be a trick to lure us into the Neutral Zone. If no distressed freighter exists, the Federation would look very bad."

Wesley bit a knuckle and said, "And what if the

Mayday is genuine? Mr. Picard, lay in a course for the freighter."

"Captain," Picard said, "the Romulans will interpret our incursion into the Neutral Zone as a hostile act."

"I am aware of that, Mr. Picard. Lay in the course."

"Aye, sir."

On the tactical display, the proposed course of the *Enterprise* was an elegant black curve from its present position to that of the *Kobayashi Maru.*

Wesley was feeling a little more comfortable with command. Everybody was cooperating. The power he felt seemed to be rising from the center seat itself. "Execute course," he said.

"Aye."

On the tactical display, the blue pulse of *Enterprise* crossed through the open mesh of the Neutral Zone limit. A few seconds later the amber light went out and the distress signal stopped in mid-word. Wesley knew he'd been had.

"Captain," said Data. "Boogeyman war spiders uncloaking *now."*

"On visual."

The tactical display was replaced by two large black ships. Each had a central button—obviously living and control quarters—from which descended three legs. At the end of each leg was a small warp engine. The war spiders were bearing down on the *Enterprise* at a high rate of speed.

Wesley cried, "Mr. Data, red alert. Get us out of here, Mr. Picard."

The red alert Klaxon began.

"Impossible, Captain. View aft." Behind the *Enterprise* were two more war spiders. The ship shuddered.

"View forward," Data said, and the picture changed just in time for them to see a photon torpedo, or something like it, fired from one of the war spiders.

"Damage report."

"Primary shield breached," Data said. "Hull damage in sections seventeen through twenty-four and thirty-six through forty. Casualties heavy."

Sweating now, Wesley looked at the back of Picard's neck. What would he do in these circumstances? Would Picard have allowed himself to get into a situation like this? "Recommendations," he said. This was supposed to be a training mission, of course. It wasn't real. Let him be trained.

"At this point, Captain—" Picard said.

He was interrupted by the hiss of an alien transporter beam. Wesley watched with morbid fascination as two beings took form on the bridge. They were the most frightening things he'd ever seen. Each of the Boogeymen was short, no taller than a human eight-year-old, and each wore a long inverted-bowl-shaped coat that fell from a tight collar, making them look almost as wide as they were tall. Their heads were round and covered with wild black hair and beards. They had stubby horns and wide snaggly teeth.

One of the Boogeymen slid forward on hidden feet, brandishing something that looked like a lump of wood but was probably a weapon. "Surrender," the Boogeyman said in a hideous, rasping parody of a human voice. "Or all will die."

"Freeze program," Wesley said.

The Boogeymen froze. The telltale at the bottom of

the main viewscreen stopped halfway across. The incoming damage control reports and the red alert Klaxon halted.

Data and Picard turned to look at Wesley with inquisitive expressions.

Wesley said, "What did I do wrong?"

Picard shook his head. "You did nothing wrong. No one has ever triumphed over the *Kobayashi Maru* scenario."

Data said, "Though legend has it that about eighty years ago, certain cadets fought it to a standstill."

"Legend," Picard said scornfully. "Academy scuttlebutt. The *Kobayashi Maru* is a no-win scenario—a test of character. Mr. Crusher did admirably. He did the only thing a moral captain could do. The fact that he was overwhelmed is unimportant."

"Thank you, sir."

"Would you care to try another scenario?" Picard asked.

To him, Picard sounded hopeful, but Wesley'd had quite enough testing of his abilities for one day. Despite the captain's kind words, Wesley needed some time to accept the fact that he wasn't an oaf for having allowed the *Kobayashi Maru* to beat him.

Picard nodded and Wesley said, "Save program and discontinue."

Wesley should have heard a tweek from the computer, and the holodeck should have gone blank. Instead, everything but the Boogeymen disappeared. Wesley and Data joined the captain. Picard had obviously taken command again, and Wesley was glad to give it to him. They circled the Boogeymen, who now had the appearance of really fine wax figures.

"Theories, Mr. Data?" Picard said.

Data shook his head. "I would have thought a malfunction on this scale would have prevented the use of the holodeck at all. Computer, explain continued existence of Boogeymen."

"Boogeymen have been saved in memory. Program has been discontinued."

"This is very odd," Picard said. "I'm sorry to do this, Mr. Crusher, but I'm certain Data can reconstruct your Boogeyman program if that seems wise. Computer, erase Boogeyman program."

"Erasing," the computer said.

"They're still there," Wesley said.

"Yes," said Picard. "Computer, exit."

To Wesley's relief, the doorway in the holodeck wall opened. Picard led the way back into the corridors of the real *Enterprise.* The holodeck doors closed behind them.

Wesley had not taken ten steps when three Boogeymen leapt from a side corridor and began to menace them with hand weapons.

Chapter Four

THE BOOGEYMEN pocketed their weapons and rushed Picard, Data, and Wesley. One of the Boogeymen got his knobby hands on Wesley, who did his best not to scream. The Boogeyman smelled of all things that were putrid and disgusting, and his skin felt the way a slug looked.

As Wesley wrangled with the Boogeyman, who was certainly much stronger than he appeared, he heard Picard call for Security. Instead of the comforting voice of Mr. Worf, Wesley heard no response at all. With the help of Data, he managed to break free from the Boogeyman. The captain and the two of them ran for a turbolift with the Boogeymen close behind. The turbolift doors closed in the faces of the Boogeymen, and Picard cried, "Bridge."

Picard and Wesley stood there breathing hard. Unperturbed but wildly interested, Data said, "That was most unusual."

61

Picard said, "It was more than unusual, Mr. Data. It was impossible. Unless Mr. Crusher is hiding a breakthrough from us, it is not possible for holodeck constructs to exist outside the holodeck."

Embarrassed and horrified by his Boogeymen, Wesley said, "No breakthroughs, sir."

"You look unwell," Data said.

"I'll be fine. But I think this is all my fault."

"Turbolift," Picard called out, "temporary halt."

The turbolift stopped, but its mechanism continued to hum around them.

Data said, "I cannot allow you to take full responsibility, Wesley. After all, I used the Borders scale to design the Boogeymen."

"Sure. To my specifications."

Picard said, "Gentlemen, please. At the moment, laying blame is not as important as finding a solution to our problem. Empirical observation forces us to make certain assumptions. Either we must admit the possibility of what we know to be impossible, or—"

"Or," Data said, "we must assume we are still on the holodeck."

"But we left the holodeck," Wesley said. The captain was right about not having time for recriminations, but that did not prevent Wesley from feeling guilty. If they ever got out of this, he'd have to find some way to apologize and, more important, make sure nothing like this ever happened again.

Considering, Data said, "We left a holodeck simulation of the bridge and entered an area that looked like a ship's corridor. Is it not possible that one is as unreal as the other?"

They contemplated that possibility for a few minutes. Wesley was glad to be on the turbolift. It gave him a certain amount of security, even if it was as fake as everything else apparently was.

"Your hypothesis is easily tested," Picard finally said. He called out, "Arch."

Before them an arch appeared. It looked like a slice of corridor. Using it, they could adjust the holodeck computer without leaving the holodeck. Picard said, "If you would be so kind, Mr. Data," and gestured toward the touch pad.

Data walked under the arch and said, "Computer." There was the familiar auditory twinkle and Data continued, "Tell me the present locations of Captain Picard, Ensign Crusher, and Commander Data."

The computer said, "They are in turbolift seven between decks three and four."

Picard looked unhappy, which was how Wesley supposed he himself looked. Picard said, "Computer. Exit holodeck."

Holodeck doors appeared in the turbolift wall. The three men stared at them skeptically.

Wesley said, "I guess we can't trust the computer."

"We can trust only ourselves," Picard said. Neither he nor Wesley stepped toward the exit. Beyond it beckoned a normal-looking corridor. It seemed to be empty.

"Shall we go?" Data said.

Picard said, "There is no guarantee that the corridor before us is any more real than the one from which we just escaped."

"And more Boogeymen could be waiting around the corner."

Data frowned. He said, "Our choice is clear. We can

either stay here for the rest of our lives, or we can search for a solution to our problem."

"Right you are, Mr. Data." Picard strode forward, Wesley and Data a few feet behind him. Suddenly three Boogeymen leapt out at the captain. He managed to twist away from them, and they went after Wesley and Data.

As he fought, Wesley felt himself losing control of his emotions. He cried with fear and frustration. Data stunned one of the Boogeymen with a roundhouse punch, and Picard used a two-handed fist to knock away the one harassing Wesley. Someone was pulling Wesley along, and then they were back inside a turbolift. He leaned against a wall, shaking.

"Emergency hold between decks three and four," Picard said. The turbolift began to move, but stopped a short time later.

"Are you all right, Mr. Crusher?" Picard said.

Wesley tried to stand up straight. He smiled and blinked and said, "I guess I shouldn't have designed them to resemble creatures I had nightmares about when I was a little kid."

Picard looked surprised, then gave Wesley an understanding smile and said, "You're to be commended for wanting to meet your ancient fears head on." He shrugged. "Though perhaps these were not the best circumstances for it." Picard seemed uncomfortable. Was it because of the situation or because of Wesley's brief breakdown? He stood up straighter and said, "I'm fine now, sir."

"Right. Computer, take us to the bridge."

The turbolift began to move again. Picard said, "Any idea what to expect, Data?"

"None whatsoever, sir. To guess without information seems pointless."

The turbolift stopped, and the doors hissed open. Picard stepped onto the bridge and fell into a martial arts crouch. Three Boogeymen were in the command seats. The one in the center jumped up and cried, "Intruders! Get them!" The other two ran toward the turbolift.

Picard pushed Wesley and Data back into the turbolift as he retreated. The doors closed and Picard said, "Deck ten."

Data said, "The main computer, sir?"

"Yes. It may be no more real than the arch, but it still may be able to tell us something about this holo-universe. Also, I'm hoping that somehow we can break through to the real *Enterprise*. How are you getting on, Mr. Crusher?"

"All right, sir." Sure. As right as can be expected when meeting one of your worst fears in the flesh. The captain was correct: it was unfortunate Wesley had used an old nightmare as the model for the aliens. But Wesley was a lot older now than when he'd had those terrible dreams. He'd designed the Boogeymen in the form of his old nightmares because he'd been convinced he could successfully face them. Having seen them, he was shaky but optimistic.

The corridor on deck ten was as deserted as the others they'd been on. Ten Forward was deserted. Not even any Boogeymen were in sight. That had to mean something. Wesley thought about this as they walked quickly to the main computer.

Every so often Picard stopped, touched a companel, and asked it where they were. None of the companels worked and Picard wondered why, if the turbolifts and the arch worked.

Data said, "Difficult to say, Captain, not knowing exactly what is wrong with the holodeck computer."

The captain kept trying. This holo-*Enterprise* looked like his ship, and at some primal level, down in the base of his brain, Wesley thought Picard still believed that it *was* his ship. The components ought to work even though all his logic told him there was no chance.

Hoping to redeem himself in Picard's eyes, Wesley said, "Sir, have you noticed how deserted the ship seems to be?"

"Not deserted enough," Picard said.

"Even the Boogeymen," Wesley said. "We've never seen more than three at a time."

Data said, "The number may be coincidental. Or it may be the result of a glitch in the program. It may mean nothing at all."

"Everything is evidence," Picard said.

"I was not disputing that fact. I was merely suggesting that the evidence may not be helpful."

Picard touched a companel and said, "Picard to Riker."

A moment passed, and Wesley thought this companel was as dead as all the others Picard had tried. Then a voice said, "Riker here, Captain." The voice could have been Riker's. Wesley smiled and even Data brightened.

"Number One, Commander Data and Ensign Crusher and I are trapped on holodeck three. Have Mr. La Forge attempt to shut down the holodeck computer." He glanced around and said, "And just to be on the safe side, send Mr. Worf with a contingent of security guards."

"Security guards?"

"Difficult to explain, Number One."

"Aye, Captain. Security guards."

As Picard stepped back from the companel to let it know he was done, he said to Data, "Perhaps you can reach the main computer through this companel."

Data stepped forward, touched the panel, and said, "Computer."

There was no response. Data called the computer again, and once more nothing happened. "Most puzzling," Data said. "Perhaps the panel is able to act only as a person-to-person communication device." He touched the companel again and said, "Data to La Forge."

Before La Forge had a chance to answer—if the companel had made contact at all—they heard scuffling behind them. In a moment, three more Boogeymen galloped down on them wearing the uniforms of *Enterprise* security guards.

In a hellish parody of Worf's voice, the lead Boogeyman cried, "Security detail reporting!"

By that time Wesley and the others were moving quickly, running around the large curve of the corridor. Wesley ran without looking back. He supposed Picard and Data were close behind him. He glanced over his shoulder, turned cold, and did what he thought was impossible—he ran faster. Two Boogeymen were chasing him. One was bald and wearing a red uniform. The other was a pale waxy yellow and wore a gold uniform. They were catching up. The bald one cried, "Mr. Crusher! Mr. Crusher!"

Wesley ran so fast he was certain he almost attained warp one. Then somebody grabbed him. He fought blindly, thrashing out and kicking and clawing, in his frenzy having forgotten everything he'd learned about martial arts.

"Mr. Crusher!"

It was Captain Picard's voice. His real voice. Wesley opened his eyes and saw that the real Captain Picard held him by both shoulders.

"Captain! They're after me. Boogeyman versions of you and Data."

Data looked back along the corridor, and said, "The corridor is empty, Wesley."

Wesley looked too, and when he saw that Data was right, he felt both relieved and cheated. He'd been ready for a fight, and now it seemed there was not to be one. He tried to make his heart stop banging quite so hard. He said, "How did you two get in front of me?"

"I wasn't aware that we were until you ran into us," Picard said.

"Evidently," said Data, "the topology of this holodeck *Enterprise* follows different rules from those on the real ship."

"Or anywhere else," said Wesley. He commanded himself to get a grip. He'd made a mistake designing the Boogeymen the way he had, and now he had to live with it. The situation would not improve if he became hysterical.

Picard looked around as if he could see the anomalies on all sides. "I'd be very surprised if the holo-*Enterprise* follows any rules at all other than the ones the Boogeymen make up as they go along."

Wesley shook his head. "They could have caught me, sir."

Picard nodded and said, "I assume you designed them to be good game players."

"Yes, sir."

"Then I suggest to you that, for whatever reason, they wish the game to continue."

That was certainly an explanation, but it didn't comfort Wesley. He'd had enough of this game already. And he'd learned a lesson about writing special programs for the holodeck.

Data said, "Perhaps the main computer core will give us more answers."

"Yes," said Picard. "And allow us to get through to the ship. Stay close, everyone."

They continued down the corridor and stopped at the entrance to the main computer core. It had double security locks, and from the look of the twin red telltales, both locks were working. Crew members did not ordinarily enter the computer core control center, and those who did required a top security clearance.

Picard set his fingertips against a blue plate, and the computer said, "Ensign Jean-Luc Picard is not cleared for this area."

Picard stepped back as if he'd been physically assaulted.

Data said, "Of course. The holodeck computer is still running Ensign Crusher's program. As far as it is concerned, Wesley is the captain."

Wesley was embarrassed by this, but Picard laughed and said, "Well then, perhaps Captain Crusher would be so kind as to put his fingers on the identity plate."

Smiling with embarrassment, Wesley did as Picard had done. The computer said, "Captain Wesley Crusher is identified."

"Open control center."

The computer thought about that for a while. Confirmation of Wesley's access to the control center should have taken nanoseconds, a time seemingly instantaneous by human clocks. "Maybe—" Wesley began.

The computer said, "Clearance confirmed," and the heavy-duty double doors slid open. The security field sparked once—which was odd—and went off.

At Picard's insistence, Wesley led them into a dim room so full of blinking lights that Wesley thought of the stars outside. Outside the holodeck. Outside the real *Enterprise*. Each light was an isolinear chip that was in use.

Four crouching dwarfs faced a thick column that ran from floor to ceiling and throbbed with its own glow, like a big heart—which, in a sense, it was. Without the main computer core, and one like it in the engineering hull, the *Enterprise* would have been nothing more than an expensively furnished rations can. It would have needed ten times its present crew working constantly just to do the routine jobs the computer did effortlessly and without bother.

Opposite the door was a flow chart showing which parts of the main computer and its satellite computer were busy and what they were doing. Had someone made an inquiry? Was someone using a food slot? Was the life-support computer making routine adjustments? The computers could do thousands of complex tasks, both independent and interconnected, and if you knew how to read the flow chart, you could find out what they were at any particular moment.

Except for the long breathe sound of the air recirculators, the room was completely silent.

Wesley said, "Raise illumination to daytime level."

The light came up, and Wesley saw that the dwarfs were computer terminals. He knew they should have been terminals, but he was relieved they weren't Boogeymen. He and Picard and Data spread out a little as they ventured farther into the room.

Picard said, "It all looks astonishingly normal."

"The computer has every inch of the ship in permanent read-only memory," Data said.

"Let's remember that when considering the Boogeymen."

Wesley sat at one of the terminals. Everyone on the ship had at least a basic knowledge of how to operate a computer, and Wesley's knowledge went far beyond the basic. Once, while on a routine mission from Starbase 123 to a nearby planet, Picard had allowed him to temporarily reprogram the navigational computer with his own set of specifications, laboriously worked out over the preceding months. The *Enterprise* had arrived three days late and fifteen planetary diameters off course, but Riker claimed to have been astonished at such sharpshooting. Picard had gently suggested Wesley reinstall the Starfleet specs.

Still, when Wesley put one hand out to the control surface, he pulled it back without touching anything. This wasn't a real terminal. It might not work at all, or it might work in a wonky way. He figured he'd caused enough trouble already. Let Data and the captain do the experimenting.

"You know why we're here, Mr. Data?" Picard asked.

The captain stood near the central column. Data had been wandering around the walls, apparently checking the chips, and then had spent some time studying the flow chart. He turned to the captain. "I do, sir. You wish me to go on line with the holo-simulation of *Enterprise's* main computer."

"Isn't that dangerous?" Wesley said. "I mean, if the main computer has an information surge while Data's on line, it could overload his circuits and blow out his positronic brain."

Matter-of-factly, Data said, "The odds of that happening are only one in eight hundred million."

"That's for the real main computer."

"The chance must be taken."

"Mr. Crusher is correct, Data. A large element of risk is involved here. That is why I am making a request rather than giving an order. Maybe we can solve our problem another way."

"I would be delighted to hear any suggestion."

"Mr. Crusher?" Picard said.

In the quiet room, Wesley tried to think of something they might do other than talk to the main computer. The main computer ran everything. It knew every centimeter and circuit of everything on the *Enterprise,* every centimeter and circuit even of itself. The main computer had to be an important part of any simulation of the *Enterprise,* and it was not impossible that the computer was simulated down to its last chip. Wesley said, "No, sir. If we're going to break through to the outside at all, this is the place to do it."

Picard nodded and said, "Very well. Proceed when ready, Mr. Data." He sat down at one of the other terminals, made as if to rest his hand on it, glanced at Wesley, who was sitting with his hands in his lap, and decided to sit that way also. Wesley didn't feel like such a gazebo if Picard also seemed to be afraid to touch anything.

Data removed a patch of his scalp to reveal an intricate web of thin silver paths and tiny blinking lights. In the center of the web was a complex computer outlet. He took a short optical cable from a storage locker and plugged one end into the outlet. To one side of the flow chart was a panel of ports into which one could plug anything from a tricorder to a single iso-linear chip. Data found a port that would fit the off-end of the optical cable, and looked back at Picard and Wesley.

"When ready, Mr. Data," Picard said.

Data nodded. Like a man delivering the final thrust of a sword, Data plugged himself into the wall. His eyes got wide, but he stood without moving.

"Do you think—" Wesley said.

Picard interrupted. "I don't know."

A low hum began. It grew in pitch and intensity. Data started to shiver. As the hum grew, he shook harder until his boots beat against the floor. Without thinking about the danger to Data or himself, Wesley rushed him and hit him hard with his shoulder, knocking him loose from the port. At the moment of impact, Wesley felt an electrical charge shoot through his body. For a moment Data lay beneath him as still as death. Wesley was not certain that he could move either.

Then Wesley felt hands under his arms, and Picard helped him to his feet. Wesley was relieved that the residual shimmer of the lightning bolt was fading. He and Picard looked down at Data. His eyes were open, but seemingly sightless, focused on nothing.

Picard knelt and called to Data. Without moving anything but his mouth, Data said, "Most interesting."

The captain shared a smile with Wesley and said, "What is most interesting, Data?"

"I believe I have just experienced a sensation humans call 'stunned.' To be dazed or bewildered. To be shocked, startled, jolted—"

"I think he's all right, sir," Wesley said.

He and Picard helped Data to his feet. Data slid the covering tip back onto his pinky and said, "Most interesting, Captain. Our analysis of the situation is correct in all important aspects. Wesley's Boogeymen have taken control of the holodeck satellite of the real *Enterprise*'s main computer. This computer"—he indicated the holodeck simulation of the main computer—"has no knowledge of any ship outside the simulation we are trapped in and therefore refuses to communicate with anyone or anything outside."

Data and Wesley looked at Picard. He appeared grim, but he shrugged and almost smiled when he said, "Then let us hope Commander Riker is taking measures to rescue us. Meanwhile, I, for one, do not propose we sit around waiting for him." He called out, "Exit holodeck."

A doorway appeared in the middle of the room, cutting into the central column. Outside was an apparently normal *Enterprise* corridor. Wesley and the others knew better, of course, but that was what it looked like.

Picard walked to the doorway and turned. "Coming, gentlemen?"

Wesley and Data followed him through the doorway.

Chapter Five

RIKER WAS HAVING a drink with Baldwin in Ten Forward when the call came through from La Forge. They sat on the highest level, the one farthest from the bar, and Baldwin was staring out the window at the rainbow streaks of stars falling toward them.

Riker sipped his transporter, a silver drink whose shimmering bubbles gave it its name. He said, "You must have formed some conclusions about the Tantamon Four natives, having been there for six months."

"Am I still on company time?" Baldwin said without turning his head.

"Sorry," said Riker, obviously a little miffed. "I was just making conversation."

Baldwin looked at him and smiled. "That's okay. I don't really mind. Exology is my life."

"You don't sound serious."

They both watched a pretty yeoman cross the room and sit down at a table with a friend.

"I almost never do. A playful attitude protects me from the stuff that really bothers me."

The pretty yeoman laughed. Light caught in her blond hair glowed.

When Riker looked back at him, Baldwin was frowning. "Thinking about Mont?" Riker said.

"I guess I was, at that. I was thinking that it's funny how you can make enemies without even half trying."

Riker nodded and looked out the window.

"Commander Riker?"

Riker touched his insignia and said, "Riker here. What is it, La Forge?"

"I have a strange power fluctuation on holodeck three. Nothing to worry about, but I thought you should know."

"Strange how?"

"It looks like signal interference, but that's not possible. Nothing on board broadcasts a signal of that type."

"The captain's using holodeck three with Data and Wesley. Is there any danger?"

"Not at the moment. But if it gets much worse, the simulation they're using will start to break up. They may suffer some disorientation."

"Let me know if the situation changes."

"Aye, sir. La Forge out."

Baldwin said, "One damn thing after another, eh, Commander?"

"Sometimes I think certain people attract trouble."

Baldwin raised his glass and said, "Here's to the heroes."

Riker smiled and joined him in the toast.

Picard led Data and Wesley through the holodeck exit into a corridor of what looked like the *Enterprise*. Once again they were ambushed by Boogeymen. Picard was not gentle fighting them off. Even if they had been real and not just holodeck fever dreams, he would not have been gentle. They had adequately demonstrated their hostility. And Picard, though a man of peace, was also nobody's fool.

Data was handling his Boogeyman with his usual élan, and even Wesley, who was understandably disturbed and intimidated by his creations, seemed to be holding his own. While gripping his Boogeyman in a headlock, Picard shouted, "Exit holodeck."

A holodeck exit opened before him. He, Data, and Wesley pushed the Boogeymen aside and leapt through. The doors slammed behind them with a satisfying bang, locking in—out?—the Boogeymen.

They stood just outside the holodeck. A few feet away was the cross corridor from which the Boogeymen usually attacked. Picard said, "Exit holodeck," and another doorway opened before them. They stepped through and found themselves in a place very much like the one they'd left. Picard said, "Exit holodeck," and they stepped through again. Hoping that the computer would just give up and allow them to exit for good and all, Picard called for the exit again. And again. He lost count of the number of times he and his companions walked through an exit to find themselves where they'd started. They developed a rhythm. Walking the same six feet over and over again was, in its bizarre way, intoxicating. But eventually it just seemed pointless.

As they stood resting in front of a holodeck door, Data said, "I fear your actions will be fruitless, Captain."

Picard smiled grimly and said, "Are you about to remind me that computers never tire or get bored?"

Data looked a little surprised. "Yes, Captain. I was."

"At least we're getting our exercise," Wesley said.

Picard knew that Wesley was responsible for their predicament, but he did not hold that against him. Not every experiment could be a success. Picard was certain that having to confront one's childhood fears over and over again could not be easy, but Wesley seemed to be making the best of it. He would log the exemplary performance of both Ensign Crusher and Commander Data. He contemplated the space around them, so familiar, and yet as alien as the backside of Borgus.

"You're right, of course, Mr. Data. And yet, waiting here seems no more constructive than walking through the same door over and over again. We are, as Mr. Crusher points out, at least getting our exercise."

Data was about to reply when his eyebrows went up. Picard had never seen him so surprised, and in fact hadn't known that he was capable of showing such a strong reaction. Picard followed his gaze and the gaze of Wesley Crusher and suddenly was at least as surprised as either of them.

Standing at the intersection of the corridors was a tall, slim woman with short blond hair. She wore a

Starfleet uniform. It was Tasha Yar, chief of security aboard *Enterprise* before her death at the metaphorical hands—the thing had no actual hands—of an amorphous tarry monster that called itself Armus.

"Tasha," Data said quietly. It was an open secret that Yar and Data had been very close under peculiar circumstances, causing much speculation—some of it less scientific than vulgar. Data claimed that, being a machine, he had no emotions. Evidently his circuits were working overtime simulating them. He looked bewildered, but pleasantly so, like a man surprised by a birthday party thrown in his honor.

Lieutenant Yar was—had been—a serious woman, but at the moment, the small nervous movements of her lips meant that she was trying not to smile.

Picard was aware—as Data and Mr. Crusher certainly must have been—that the Yar before them was a hologram, no more real than the Boogeymen. Still, the effect was startling, and wishful thinking made it necessary for Picard to continually remind himself that she wasn't real. Crusher looked at Picard for a clue as to how to act.

From the side of his mouth, Picard said, "The Boogeymen may have made their first mistake. If this Lieutenant Yar is as sympathetic as the real one would have been under these circumstances, we may have found our way into the main computer and from there a way out."

"I believe you are correct, Captain," Data said. "I will attempt to speak with her. It. Her." He walked forward and stood within easy reach of her. "It is good to see you again, Lieutenant."

Yar said, "Good to see you, too. Still fully functional?"

"Of course."

This time Yar allowed herself a smile. It was as radiant as the smile of the original. Wesley whispered, "Hard to believe she's not real."

Picard nodded and raised a hand for silence.

Data said, "If you are a fabrication of the holodeck computer, you certainly know our problem."

"Of course."

"And perhaps a solution?"

"Of course. If you, Captain Crusher, and Mr. Picard will follow me, I'll show it to you."

Data glanced back and Picard nodded. Softly, he said, "Look sharp, everyone. This may be a trap." Yar and Data set off down the hall together with Picard and Wesley following.

As they walked, Wesley said, "Sorry about that 'captain' stuff, sir."

Picard said, "If everything and everybody on the holodeck thinks this is the real *Enterprise* and that you are the captain, perhaps the misdirection will work in our favor."

Something fell onto Picard like a bag full of rocks. It knocked him off his feet, and in a moment a man was bending over him with his hands around Picard's throat.

Ninja, Picard thought with the calm part of his mind. Must have been hanging from the ceiling like a spider. The attacker's ill-fitting outfit, including a hood and a swatch across his mouth, was the same neutral brown in which much of the ship was decorated. While he thought this, Picard grabbed the cloth covering the ninja's stomach with both hands and rolled backward, slamming the ninja's head into the deck, knocking him out. While watching the ninja for signs of returning consciousness, Picard leapt to his feet and cried, "Exit holodeck!"

With clever use of his fists and legs, Data had knocked his own ninja to the deck, and Wesley was poking his ninja in the face with the outstretched fingers of one hand while he punched with the other.

Picard hustled them through the exit and looked back briefly. Yar stood among the three unconscious ninjas and gave him a mock salute. The holodeck door hissed closed. "Nightmares about ninjas, Mr. Crusher?" Picard asked.

"No, sir. Maybe the Boogeymen just pulled them out of the memory bank because ninjas are good fighters."

Picard nodded. Wesley's explanation might even be correct. When the captain turned, he saw that Data was still looking at the holodeck door.

Picard said, "That wasn't really Lieutenant Yar."

"I know," said Data. "Still, it does seem a shame that an image that looks so much like her would be so deceitful."

"Captain," said Wesley, "where are we?"

Picard and Data stopped staring glumly at the door and took note of their surroundings. They were certainly no longer aboard the *Enterprise,* not even a holodeck version. They were in a small office whose walls were covered with faded flowered paper. Over a battered green filing cabinet hung a calendar featuring a flat photograph of a running horse. A very old wooden desk stood in front of an even older swivel chair. From the window near the desk they could look down onto a noisy street crowded with vehicles powered by internal combustion engines. Across from the desk, on a threadbare rug, stood a wooden armchair that had been loved too little, and beyond that was a door inset with a big pebbled-glass window. From behind the door came the sound of uncertain typing. The warm air smelled of cooking grease and incompletely burned fossil fuel.

Picard knew exactly where they were. They were in the office of a private investigator, a shamus, a gumshoe, a hard-boiled detective. They were also in a bad situation, so Picard tried not to enjoy being where he was. He tried and failed dismally. The Boogeymen and the holodeck computer, for reasons of their own, had put him and Data and Wesley right in the middle of one of his favorite fantasies.

Picard said, "We're in the office of Dixon Hill."

"Who?" Wesley said.

"A mid-twentieth century detective," Picard said. "In business for himself. A white knight who walks the mean streets to protect the innocent and ferret out the guilty."

While he explained, Picard strolled to the filing cabinet and took a brown fedora from the top drawer. He put it on and adjusted it in a mirror over a tiny washstand. He put on the trench coat that hung from the hat rack.

"And," said Data, "a character who is entirely fictional."

"No more or less fictional than Sherlock Holmes."

"Point well taken, sir," said Data as he nodded.

Someone knocked on the door. Picard glanced at the other two. The swivel chair complained bitterly as he sat down behind his desk; Data and Wesley took up positions on either side of him. "Come in," Picard said.

A tall, slim woman came in and leaned against the door she'd just closed. Her dress was made of a loud floral print and was tight as the skin of a peach. Her hairstyle was a frothy thing Picard did not recognize but was probably right for Dixon Hill's era. She said, "A woman is here to see you."

"A customer?" Picard said.

"Probably. She's a looker. You'll want to see her alone." The woman glanced meaningfully at Data and Wesley.

"Don't worry about that," said Picard. "Shoo her in, Effie. Shoo her in."

The moment they were alone, Data said, "Is it wise to get involved in a holodeck scenario at this time, sir?"

Earnestly, Picard said, "The Boogeymen are presenting this to us for a reason. Finding out what it is will certainly tell us something."

"It might be another trap," Wesley said.

Picard heard Wesley's intake of breath, and when he looked toward the door, Picard could not help making the same noise.

Posed in the frame of the doorway was one of the most striking women Picard had ever seen. She rivaled even the women of his student days in Paris.

The fact that she made Effie look like a boy was no insult to either of them.

She was a redhead to make a priest think twice. Her high-heeled green shoes matched her tailored suit and brought out the color of her eyes. Her mouth was red and inviting. After long study, Picard noted that her stockings were very sheer indeed. Under her arm was a chocolate brown purse large enough to hold the evening papers, and on her head was a green hat that looked as if it had been folded from a desk blotter. Her teardrop earrings might have been dipped from the ocean on a clear day.

The woman said, "Mr. Hill?"

Picard's impulse was to leap up and help the woman into the customer's chair, but that wouldn't have been the detective way. He said, "Who's asking?"

The woman managed to get into the customer's chair all by herself. She crossed her astonishing legs, leaned toward him, and said, "My name is Rhonda Howe, and I am in very big trouble."

"It's a good day for it, Miss Howe," Picard said.

Rhonda Howe glanced at Data and Wesley and said, "I thought you worked alone."

"This is as alone as it gets. Tell me about your problem."

"Very well." Picard enjoyed watching her get comfortable in the chair. She said, "I'm being harassed by some rather unpleasant men. They are all short and wear dark clothing. They have lots of shaggy hair, and I think they have horns."

"Horns?"

"It's hard to tell with all that hair."

"Of course," Picard said. "Why not call the police?"

"The Howe family insists on privacy and gets it."

"Have you offered money to these unpleasant men?" Picard said.

He didn't think it was possible to make Rhonda Howe blush, but she blushed then like a sunrise in the Adirondacks. "I don't think it's money they're interested in."

Picard thought of a few clever rejoinders for that, but under the trench coat and fedora he was still a starship captain, and starship captains did not make certain kinds of jokes under any circumstances.

Picard stood up and ushered Rhonda Howe to the door. "It'll be just a few minutes while I discuss this with my operatives." He closed the door and, with his hand still on the knob, let out a sigh.

"Wow," said Wesley softly.

Data said, "If by your responses you mean Rhonda Howe is an exceptionally beautiful woman, I agree with you."

Picard looked at Data, eyebrows up in question.

Data said, "I meant only that she bears an astonishing resemblance to certain High Renaissance Madonnas."

"Of course," said Picard. "The question is, should we take her case?"

Wesley said, "Sounds as if she has Boogeyman trouble."

"Wesley's right, sir. I believe your instincts were correct when you chose to get involved in this scenario. We must take her case and defeat the Boogeymen once and for all if we can."

"If we can?" Wesley said.

"Just a figure of speech," Data said.

"Very well," Picard said. He tipped a key on a brown wooden box and said, "Send in Miss Howe."

Effie's voice came through the box, a tinny shadow of itself. "Yes, sir."

Miss Howe came back into the office and settled herself in the customer's chair. She was so completely sexual a creature that sensuality shone through her most innocent movement like the sun behind a stained-glass window.

Picard said, "We've decided to take your case."

"How wonderful. Can you come to the mansion today?"

"I believe we have nothing else on the schedule."

Miss Howe smiled, and Picard said, "Freeze program." It was a nice smile, Picard thought, worth looking at a little longer.

"If the computer will freeze the program, maybe we don't have to fight the Boogeymen," Wesley said.

"We have been fooled before."

"Exit," said Picard.

A holodeck exit opened in a side wall. Beyond was an empty *Enterprise* corridor. Picard touched his insignia and called for Number One. No answer came. Data and Wesley called Riker with the same negative result. Picard said, "Is it possible that all three of our communicators are inoperative?"

"Possible," said Data, "but unlikely in the extreme."

"Then the question becomes: Do we want to escape from this particular scenario?"

"I think not, sir. I believe we should wait and see what the Boogeymen have planned."

"I concur entirely. Computer."

"Waiting," the computer said.

"Continue scenario at the Howe mansion."

Picard heard the computer's audio twinkle, and suddenly the four of them were standing in the two-story foyer of a magnificent twentieth-century home. The room was bigger than the bridge, smaller than Engineering, and rather old-fashioned, even for the time of Dixon Hill. The walls were highly polished wood panels between which hung tapestries depicting royal deer hunts. On the shiny floor were throw rugs the size of other people's rooms. At the far end wide stairways came down from a second-floor gallery on either side of a fireplace that was constructed from boulders.

Rhonda Howe said, "It was so good of you to come all the way out here. My room is upstairs."

"Your room?" Picard said.

"Where I was menaced by those awful men. I thought you might want to look for clues."

With her large green eyes she watched him hopefully. Picard tried not to fall into them. He said, "You thought right. Lead the way."

Picard, Data, and Wesley followed her across the foyer, their shoes ticking against the tessellated floor, silent against the thick rugs. When Miss Howe had one foot on the bottom step, a very tall man entered the foyer through a side door. White hair was swept back above his ears like wings, and a wispy white beard grew from his chin. He was dressed in a cutaway coat and striped pants. He bowed no more than he had to and in a deep resonant voice said, "Excuse me, Miss Rhonda, but your father would like to see Mr. Hill."

As if really concerned, she said, "Can it wait? Mr. Hill is busy right now."

"Your father is most insistent."

Picard said, "You three go ahead. I trust my operatives implicitly, Miss Howe." While she, Data, and Wesley continued up the stairs, Picard followed the butler back through the side door and along a passage lined with heavily laden bookshelves. They went through an entrance that could only have been a primitive airlock, and into an enormous greenhouse. Picard immediately began to sweat.

The butler said, "Watch your step, sir. Creepers."

Aside from a sweat bath, this was the warmest room Picard had ever been in. He fanned himself with his hat as the butler led him along a winding brick path among the trees, bushes, and winding vines of a tropical forest. Fat drops of moisture fell from everything, including the butler and Picard. A sickly sweetness of too much perfume weighed down the air. Pale green light filtered through tentatively from the glass roof above.

In an open area a very old man sat in a wheelchair staring out through a glass wall at rolling grassy hills. Near him was a white iron table with a white telephone on it and a white iron chair next to it. A shawl was draped across the man's shoulders, and a rug was thrown across his knees. The man looked like the bitter end of a life that had not been easy. Hands like unbaked dough plucked at the rug. His face was no more than many pouches of sagging skin crossed with tiny red and blue veins. His lips were thin and nearly the same color as the skin. Only his eyes were alive. They were the same sea green as his daughter's, and they watched Picard, appraising him as if he were a head of beef.

"Mr. Howe, Mr. Hill," the butler said, and went away. Somewhere beyond the jungle a door closed.

Mr. Howe invited Picard to sit down, and then he said, "I suppose my daughter hired you to see about her boogeymen."

The word shocked Picard. Was it possible the computer would speak with him through this holo-man rather than using its own computer voice? Carefully, Picard said, "Boogeymen?"

"Something wrong with the word? Ghost, then. Hobgoblin. Nightmare. Whatever."

The computer was playing with him. It knew the creatures Wesley had created were called Boogeymen. Using the strange double-think that computers used so well, it had fabricated a man who not only did not know a computer problem existed but was unaware of his own computer origin. Picard wondered briefly if flesh-and-blood people were any more aware of their origins or the problems of their Maker.

"You don't seem concerned," Picard said.

Mr. Howe made a noise of dismissal and said, "Like her father, she has an active imagination. Sometimes it's overactive. That's all."

"What do you expect me to do, then? Slug her

upside the head and tiptoe out while she's unconscious?"

"I don't think the slugging will be necessary. Just
tell her that we spoke and that you're leaving. You may
keep any money she paid you." He shook his head.
"It's not your fault she's a twit."

Picard remembered something Dixon Hill had said
in a book called *Sweet Oblivion*. He quoted it to Mr.
Howe: "'All I have is my good name. Imagine what
my reputation would be like if I let people who
weren't my clients run me off cases.'"

"I'm her father."

"She doesn't look like a child." Picard stood up and
said, "If nothing else, she needs to be comforted. Even
if that's all she buys, she's doing all right."

Mr. Howe studied his lap. Far away Picard heard
the airlock door open, then the sound of people
beating their way through the undergrowth. In a
moment the butler came into the clearing followed by
Rhonda Howe, Data, and Wesley.

Mr. Howe snickered and said, "Find anything?"

"How are you feeling, Dad?"

"Fine, fine. Did you find anything?"

Looking a little confused, Miss Howe said, "Nothing at all. Mr. Hill's operative, Mr. Data, thinks that's
important."

Picard nodded at Data, who said, "Wesley and I
searched Miss Howe's room and found no clues
whatsoever. We also found nothing beneath Miss
Howe's second-story window. No footprints, no torn
shrubs, nothing dropped from a pocket."

"You see?" Mr. Howe said.

Data said, "The fact we found nothing is in itself

conclusive. In this scenario, only Boogeymen would have the capability to hang outside Miss Howe's window and, as she describes it, moan at her, without leaving any clues behind."

"I don't get you," Mr. Howe said.

Data was about to explain when three Boogeymen leapt in through the wall of the greenhouse; the effect was like an explosion, pelting them with shards of glass. The two end ones were dressed in brown pin-striped suits and were waving twentieth-century projectile-spitting pistols. The one in the middle wore a gray suit and a fedora. In his whispering nightmare voice the Boogeyman in the middle said, "Captain Crusher. Captain Crusher."

Wesley backed toward the jungle, horror on his face. Picard and Data closed in front of him, their hands up, ready to do battle.

One of the hench-Boogeymen fired twice into the air, bringing a shower of broken glass down onto himself. At the same time, the chief mobster-Boogeyman burst between Picard and Data, grabbed Wesley, and threw him over one shoulder like a sack of potatoes. Seconds later, all three Boogeymen had ducked out through the jagged hole they'd made in the wall.

Data was already after Wesley and the three Boogeymen, and Picard was right behind him. He had only enough time to hear Mr. Howe comment calmly, "It's all her imagination."

The outside air seemed cold after the close heat of the greenhouse, and it refreshed Picard immediately. He threw off his trench coat and fedora as he followed Data to the first gentle rise and, not far away, saw the three Boogeymen moving along in a gorillalike crouch. One of the Boogeymen still carried Wesley over his shoulder.

"We can surely catch them," the captain said as they started down the hill.

Suddenly Picard was blinded by a flash of light.

Chapter Six

RIKER SAT in the captain's chair and did not look happy to be there. He glared at the main viewscreen, just to have something to glare at besides the shine on the toe of his left boot. On the screen stars sprinkled toward him as the *Enterprise* poked toward Memory Alpha at warp five. He turned and glared at Counselor Troi, who sat with her eyes closed. Dr. Crusher sat in the chair that Riker normally occupied. She did not glare at Troi, but waited with a look of expectation on her face. She was just as tense as Riker.

"They are confused," said Troi without opening her eyes, "and a little upset." She smiled. "No reading off Data, of course. The captain is trying hard not to be angry."

"What about?" Riker said.

"Impossible to say."

"What about Wesley?" Dr. Crusher said.

"He is bearing up well."

"That's something, I guess," Dr. Crusher said and leaned back in Riker's chair. She drummed her fingers on her thigh.

Riker called into the air, "La Forge?"

"Here, Commander," came La Forge's voice.

"Any luck getting onto the holodeck?"

"Not so far, sir. Every time we set up a bypass, the computer takes control by another route."

"Can't you override?"

"Override is inoperative."

"How about cutting through the doors?"

"Working on it now, sir. It'll take a few hours. We have to be careful where we cut. And tritanium alloy is not exactly tissue paper."

"Keep me posted."

"Aye, sir."

Riker stood up and began to pace. Dr. Crusher took another look at Troi, who shrugged apologetically. Dr. Crusher left the bridge.

The Boogeyman who'd been carrying Wesley threw him onto his bed and stood at its foot, grinning at him unpleasantly. A second sat in the chair behind his desk, and the third paced in front of the door.

This was weird, Wesley thought. Here he was in his bed seeing Boogeymen, just as if he were a kid again and in the middle of a nightmare. The difference this time was that he was awake and the Boogeymen were real now, or as real as the computer could make them. He was still afraid of them, but not the way he'd been terrorized by them in his nightmares. As far as he was concerned, these Boogeymen were just wild and unpredictable enemies. Being afraid of them seemed pretty rational.

The Boogeyman at the foot of the bed clasped his hands over his head and cried, "We win, Captain Crusher!" Something gooey and greenish yellow dripped from his teeth and into his beard.

"Right," Wesley said. "Congratulations. So the game is over. Return control of the holodeck to the computer."

"Return control?" the Boogeyman said. "We win!" He raised his hands in victory again.

The Boogeymen sounded confused, and suddenly Wesley realized why. No matter how evil they acted, the Boogeymen were still only manifestations of a computer program, and they couldn't do anything they hadn't been programmed to do. They had been designed to win and that was all. Wesley had frankly never thought the game would develop into a kidnapping. As far as he'd been concerned either he or the Boogeymen would blow the other out of the sky and then the game would be over. He'd given no thought to what might come after that, and so the Boogeymen had no idea either. They just grinned at him, dripping awful stuff.

The Boogeymen took no notice when Wesley rolled to his feet. But when he started for the door they ganged up in front of him. "We win," the one in the fedora said. Wesley had fought his share of Boogeymen by now, but he'd fought them only one at a time. He was not confident he could take on three at once. He'd probably give it a try after a while. He sat down on his bed and hoped that Picard and Data arrived before he was bored out of his mind.

Instinctively, Picard threw his hands over his eyes. When the glare was gone he blinked back tears and tried to look around through the gradually fading afterimage of sheet lightning.

"Captain," Data said, "are you all right?"

"Fine, Mr. Data." Except for the tearing and the blinking, it was true. "And you?"

"Undamaged, sir."

"Wesley?" Picard said hopefully.

No answer.

By this time Picard could see pretty well. He and Data were standing on a blank holodeck. Wesley was not there.

"Have we somehow escaped back to the ship?" Picard said.

Data said, "You assume that we are standing on the holodeck of our real *Enterprise.* I suggest that this may be a simulation of a holodeck."

Picard considered that. A holodeck simulation of a blank holodeck had its hilarious aspects, and Picard was certain that some other time he would be able to appreciate them. It was a nice complement to the wheels-within-wheels conundrum in which they found themselves—a fascinating philosophical problem, but practically, thinking about it would lead only to frustration. He shook his head. "If this is a blank holodeck, if it is the holodeck on which we played out the Dixon Hill scenario, then Wesley ought to be here."

"Correct, Captain," said Data, "which leads me to believe that we are not yet on a real holodeck. Wesley has merely been taken to another area of the simulation."

Picard looked around at the grid lines on the walls of the holodeck, broken only by a single exit. The place looked so damned real. He said, "Might walking through another holodeck exit take us to a place where we would never be able to find Wesley? Or would it lead us back out into the real ship?"

"Possibly, sir. It is more likely that a holo exit from a simulated blank holodeck would leave us in the same simulation of *Enterprise* that we are in now."

"Very well," the captain said. "In any case, it is pointless to stay here. Exit holodeck."

The doors slid open, showing an empty *Enterprise* corridor beyond. Picard and Data walked out, and the doors slid closed behind them. Picard said, "Exit holodeck," and another door appeared not six feet away. "That answers that question. Cancel exit." The door went away.

As they approached the cross corridor, three Boogeymen swarmed toward them. Bored, frustrated, very unhappy, Picard grabbed the nearest Boogeyman by the neck and slammed his head against the wall. Evidently Data was also tired of this particular method of attack because he took care of the other two Boogeymen. The three lay on the floor in an unclean heap.

"That's done with, anyway," said Picard.

"Yes, sir. Where to now?"

Indeed, that was the question. He considered all

they knew about the situation. "Let's use Occam's razor," Picard said.

"Ah," said Data. "The theory that the simplest explanation covering all the facts is the correct one." He shrugged. "It is not very scientific, but it is a place to begin."

Picard touched his insignia and got the audio twinkle. He said, "Ensign Crusher."

No answer.

"Try Captain Crusher."

Picard tried it, to the same effect.

"Still some kind of interference," Data said.

"Very well." Picard touched a companel and said, "Computer."

"Working."

"Tell me the location of Captain Wesley Crusher."

"Captain Wesley Crusher is on the main bridge."

"Why is he not answering his communicator?"

"No one has called him."

"His presence on the bridge follows the pattern," Data said. "The computer seems determined to give each of us our fondest fantasy and then pervert it. Lieutenant Yar was a traitor, and Wesley was abducted right under the nose of master sleuth Dixon Hill."

"Then Wesley could be in serious trouble."

Picard and Data hurried into a turbolift and went to the bridge. Neither of them spoke as they rode. When the turbolift slowed, they sank into martial arts crouches. The doors shushed open. Before they stepped onto the bridge, Picard peered out at it. A star field was on screen. A Boogeyman sat at the conn and another at Ops. A third sat in the center seat. They did not look up at the sound of the arriving lift.

"It all seems very placid," Picard said quietly.

"Yes, sir. Unnervingly so."

"Are you unnerved, Mr. Data?"

"Merely a metaphor. It *is* very strange."

"Take up a position at the foot of the tactical rail."

"Aye, sir."

They walked onto the bridge. Picard expected the Boogeymen to leap at them at any moment. Tension wound tighter and tighter inside him as nothing continued to happen. To be constantly vigilant could be more wearing than to be constantly in action.

He stood in front of the captain Boogeyman, blocking his view of the main screen. Still nothing happened. The Boogeyman just sat with his hands knitted across his large belly. To be ignored was maddening.

Picard said, "Where is Captain Crusher?"

The Boogeyman clasped his hands in the air and cried, "We win!"

"You win what?" Picard asked angrily.

"We win!" the Boogeyman said again with his arms raised.

Picard sighed, looked at Data, and said, "You win. End program. Abandon and exit."

Nothing happened.

Picard shook his head. "I'm out of ideas, Mr. Data."

"I have one, sir."

Picard sank into the chair normally occupied by Counselor Troi and rubbed his face with one hand.

"We might as well discuss it here as anywhere. The computer can hear us wherever we go."

"Yes, sir. I have noticed something interesting in the actions of the people we've met."

"Go on."

"The reaction time of the ninjas accompanying Lieutenant Yar was microseconds slower than I would have expected."

"Is that important?"

"I believe it is, sir. In the world of computer simulations, a microsecond is a significant period of time. The Boogeymen who abducted Wesley from the Howe greenhouse also moved slowly. As do these Boogeymen here. I might also point out that when you called for an exit while holo-people were present, the exit was noticeably late."

"All of which means what?"

"In each case, I believe the slowdown occurred because more people were generated by the holodeck computer than it could easily handle in its present weakened and polluted condition."

Picard sat up a little straighter. Perhaps there was hope yet for Wesley, for all of them. "We have never seen more than three Boogeymen at a time. And when they were with other holo-people—"

"Such as ninjas or the Howes—"

"They moved more slowly than expected. Just as the exits appeared more slowly than expected when other simulated people were present. What about them?" Picard indicated the three Boogeymen on the bridge.

Data said, "I hypothesize that they are moving

slowly because the computer has fabricated other Boogeymen who are presently with Wesley."

"Of course. Delightful. Delightful. Well done, Mr. Data. I believe you have found their Achilles' heel." Picard rubbed his chin for a moment and said, "And I believe I have thought of a way to prick it."

Chapter Seven

DR. CRUSHER SAT at her desk in sickbay turning her medical tricorder on and off. When she turned it on, the tricorder made an audible twinkle and the red power light glowed. When she turned it off, the power light went out. She watched it as if it were blinking a coded message. On. Off. On. Off.

Counselor Troi came into sickbay and sat down across from her without being asked. Troi allowed Crusher to ignore her for a while and then said, "I could feel your concern two decks from here."

"Sorry," said Dr. Crusher. She made a self-deprecating smile and turned off the tricorder again. She laid it aside with a certain finality and pressed her hands down flat on the desk. "I'm really fine," Dr. Crusher said.

"You're not fine and that's all right. Your son is missing in the depths of the holodeck and you're worried. Nothing could be more natural."

"He's with Data and the captain. He'll be fine. *I'm* fine."

Troi smiled and said, "An Earth sage once said that a doctor who treats herself has a fool for a patient."

"Booga-booga," said Crusher without humor. "How long before Geordi cuts through the door?"

"Maybe another hour. As he continues to remind us, 'tritanium alloy is not exactly tissue paper.'"

"A tissue-paper starship wouldn't be of much use to anybody."

Troi looked at the ceiling as if a tissue-paper starship were hanging there. "No, it wouldn't," she said. "Not much use. It would just be pretty."

They sat in silence for a while. Dr. Crusher's hands strayed toward the medical tricorder but didn't touch it. Troi stood up and said, "Care to join me in Ten Forward?"

Dr. Crusher frowned.

Troi smiled and said, "The ship is full of companels. And besides, Commander Riker can reach you by way of your insignia. Or my insignia. The ship is full of insignia too."

"It's office hours."

"Give yourself the same break you would prescribe to anyone else. Anybody who needs you will be able to find you."

Dr. Crusher drummed her fingers for a moment. Troi watched her, an inquisitive half smile on her face. "Right," Dr. Crusher said. She put the tricorder away and squeezed Troi's hand as they went out.

Evidently the computer had not been able to guess what Picard and Data had in mind because they arrived safely at the recreation deck. As they strode onto the large open floor, Picard said, "You might have told me before about this slowdown."

"It's only a theory, sir. Attempting to contact Wesley by companel or insignia seemed to offer more hope of success."

"Taking advantage of that slowdown is our only hope now," Picard said as he glanced around. He imagined that the large open space was filled with ghosts, all watching him, waiting for him and Data to try one more solution and fail.

The rec deck was the largest open area on the ship. With the help of the main computer, sections of the floor could be laid out for basketball, horseshoes, shuffleboard, one-thumb, almost any sport enjoyed by any species in the Federation. Even on a ship where a holodeck was available, it was sometimes important for beings to know they were playing against other beings and not against a computer simulation. Sometimes make-believe was not good enough.

At the moment, the important thing about the rec deck was that a large proportion of the *Enterprise*'s crew could meet there at one time. Such a space was necessary not only for sports but because live performances of music and drama had never quite gone out of style, despite dire warnings to the contrary ever since the invention of the moving picture in the late nineteenth century, old calendar.

Though Picard understood the need for a place like the rec deck, all that open space seemed a little unnatural on a starship. He touched a companel, got the twinkle, and said, "This is, er, Mr. Picard. Captain Crusher orders the presence of all personnel on the recreation deck. Secure your positions and come immediately."

A moment later the computer said, "Mr. Picard is not in the chain of command and therefore cannot give such an order."

"Why—" Picard began angrily, then realized that huffing and puffing at the companel would do him no good. He took a few deep breaths and said, "Mr. Data, perhaps you can do better."

"Yes, sir." Data touched the companel.

"Identify Lieutenant Commander Data," the computer said.

Data repeated Picard's order word for word.

The computer said, "Requesting the presence of all on-duty personnel is against regulations."

To Picard, Data said, "At any one time at least a third of the crew is off duty. I think that will be enough for our purposes."

"Very well."

"Computer," Data said.

"Working."

"Captain Crusher orders the presence of all off-duty personnel on the recreation deck. Immediately."

A moment later they heard the computer's voice echoing throughout the ship. It came from every companel, from the insignia of every off-duty crew member. Picard admired the computer's attempt to continue the illusion that this was the real *Enterprise*. The computer could, of course, have just made them come. Or even just made them suddenly appear. Or maybe it couldn't, Picard thought. After all, wasn't finding out things like that a point of this exercise?

Crew members arrived singly and in twos, threes, and larger groups. Though Vulcans had been serving with humans on starships for many years and members of other races had followed, Starfleet had found through hard experience that the crews of starships were generally happier if all the members came from the same race. This wasn't a value judgment—Starfleet never tried to decide if one race was better than another, but it was certain that they were all different.

Though it carried a primarily human crew, the *Enterprise* had a tradition of leavening the mix with nonhumans. Worf was a Klingon, of course—unthinkable on a Federation vessel till just recently—and Troi was half Betazoid. But there were a few Vulcans on the *Enterprise* too, most of them in the science sections. Also some Benzites with their smoking gas feeders around their necks.

That seemed like a lot of nonhumans when Picard saw them all together, but they actually accounted for much less than one percent of the crew.

Picard and Data stood to one side, watching them arrive. The first few crew members seemed to move normally, though Data said he could detect a slowdown. After the first ten or so entered the rec deck, Picard leaned over to Data and said, "Yes, I see." Even with his merely human senses, he could not help noticing that the gathering crew members were moving as if they were underwater. As more of them arrived, the ones already there slowed even more. They stood around like cadets at their first Academy dance.

"Becoming very creaky, aren't they? Almost painful to watch."

"They are not real," Data said.

"No. But they seem—"

There was a loud pop, and a bright flash filled the room. Picard lowered his arm from his eyes. Through his blinking he saw that they were once again on a blank holodeck.

"Real or simulation?" Picard said.

"Captain!" a voice cried.

He spun around and saw Wesley walking toward him and Data from a far corner.

Picard shook hands warmly with Wesley and said, "Mr. Crusher, it is good to see you again. Where have you been?"

"In my cabin, sir. Or in a simulation of my cabin, anyway. Three Boogeymen were guarding me, but I don't know what they wanted. *They* didn't know what they wanted. They knew they'd won the game, but they didn't know what to do next."

"Indeed," said Data. "The captain and I had the same problem."

Wesley looked around uncertainly. "Is this the real holodeck or just another simulation?"

Heartily, with great optimism, Picard said, "I suggest we call for an exit and find out. Computer—"

Before Picard could say more, the twin doors of the holodeck exit grated open, giving Lieutenant Commander La Forge just enough room to force his way onto the holodeck sideways. He regained his balance and smiled as he walked toward them quickly. Picard said, "Good to see you, Mr. La Forge."

"Same here, Captain. We've been trying to get onto the holodeck since we lost contact with you." La Forge looked around. "You must have been pretty bored stuck on a blank holodeck all this time. What's so funny, Wes?"

Wesley shook his head.

Picard said, "It's a long story, Mr. La Forge. Data can fill you in on any technical details. I want every holodeck on the ship sealed until we discover what's wrong with this one."

"Aye, sir."

As Data and La Forge walked off together, already deep in conversation about chips, memory capacity, computing speed, and energy flow, Wesley said, "What about me, sir?"

Picard studied Wesley for a moment, deciding how hard he should be on the boy. He said, "Go home. Think about what you've learned today, not only about computer programming but also about the dangers of doing an experiment that you have not thought through completely."

"Yes, sir," Wesley said dejectedly.

Picard almost suggested Wesley go help La Forge and Data, but he thought better of it. Wesley always enjoyed a technical problem, the more tangled the better, and no doubt he would have something to contribute. But just for the moment, Picard thought it would be better if Wesley had some time on his hands. Let him ponder his errors in judgment. Maybe he would learn something.

Picard squeezed through the partly open holodeck doors, smiled, and nodded at the crew that was cleaning up the mess La Forge had made while attempting to force the doors open. As he approached the cross corridor, he hesitated for a moment, chided himself for being silly, and walked on.

Alone aboard the turbolift, on his way to the bridge, Picard's paranoia got the better of him for a moment. He called, "Exit holodeck."

No exit appeared. The computer said, "Null command." Picard sighed.

No one was in sickbay but an orderly, who told Wesley that Dr. Crusher had gone to Ten Forward with Counselor Troi. While watching for Boogeymen he knew were not there, Wesley walked the corridors, rode the turbolift, smiled at the people. Being back in the real world was such a relief, he could barely believe he was really there.

The captain had told him to think. He would have done that anyway. Counselor Troi told him that he sometimes thought too much. His thinking went like this: Creating the Boogeymen had seemed like a good idea before, and it still did. If Wesley was to deal with the unknown, he needed more interesting adversaries than computer composites of Romulans or Ferengi. Starfleet used simulations to test their cadets. Why couldn't Wesley use them to test himself? The idea was sound.

Wesley believed that *he* could have made a programming error, but he refused to believe that Data was fallible in that way. Besides, no programming error, no matter how horrendous, could have caused the problems they'd had on the holodeck. A program so deformed would simply not run at all. No, something else was wrong. Wesley needed more facts. He'd have to join Geordi and Data.

While Wesley was on his way to Ten Forward, the turbolift shuddered, almost knocking him down. Despite his wild first thoughts, he knew the Boogeymen couldn't be the cause. This was the real *Enterprise*. Still, a malfunction of that type was unusual. He touched his insignia and called Maintenance. The crew member on duty said she'd take care of the problem. Wesley was certain she would, but he could not help worrying.

He arrived safely at deck ten and walked into Ten Forward. He stood at the door, allowing his eyes to adjust to the low light while searching for his mother. She found him first and ran across the room to hug him, embarrassing Wesley.

"Uh, hi, Mom. I'm back. Counselor Troi with you?"

Dr. Crusher backed off and looked at him fondly. "Are you all right?"

"Sure. Fine, Mom. Can we sit down? Everybody's looking at us."

"Sure. Come on."

People greeted them as they walked to the table, but the greetings were normal, not the grandiose words you would expect for somebody who'd just come back from a great adventure. A great adventure on the holodeck. That was almost a contradiction in terms.

Counselor Troi smiled at Wesley in the way that always made him wish he were a little older. "Good to see you, Wes. We were worried."

Wesley nodded, embarrassed again, this time because Troi thought he was a hero. The captain was a hero. Professor Baldwin was a hero. He was just some kid who'd gotten caught hanging a little bad input. Guinan brought Wesley a clear ether. She smiled at him, patted his shoulder, and went away. Wesley pulled the blue plastic spaceship from the clear fizzing liquid and nibbled on the cherry it impaled. As far back as he could remember, the plastic spaceships had always been green. Come on, Wesley, he told himself. The Boogeymen are gone. You're home. Give it a rest.

"Are you going to tell us about it, or do I have to tickle you the way I did when you were a child?"

"Mom!" Wesley cried, horrified.

She folded her arms on the table and sipped her drink through a straw, waiting innocently for him to begin.

Wesley told the story. Dr. Crusher and Counselor Troi listened, interrupting only to gasp in astonishment at every setback and clever solution. They laughed when Wesley told them about Rhonda Howe. Dr. Crusher said, "I'll have to remember that next time I want to get the captain's attention."

Wesley shook his head. He knew his mother and the captain were friends. He even knew his mother had an interest in the captain that went well beyond duty or even friendship. But it was difficult—impossible— for Wesley to think of her in the same way he thought of Rhonda Howe. And it was even more impossible for him to imagine the captain and his mother doing anything together they wouldn't do on the bridge.

"So how did you get out?" Dr. Crusher said. "Did Geordi save you?"

"He tried, but he was a little late." Wesley leaned toward them as if confiding a secret and smiled. "This is good," he said. He felt more comfortable talking about nuts and bolts than about feelings. "Data and Captain Picard overloaded the computer."

"How did they do that?" Dr. Crusher said.

"Data noticed that the more people the computer fabricated, the slower they moved. He and the captain guessed that if they forced it to fabricate enough people, the computer would go into overload. It would need so much memory and computing power to manifest the other people that it would be forced to overwrite the Boogeymen, which after all are just manifestations of a program."

Dr. Crusher said, "I've seen hundreds of people at a time in some of the holodeck programs I've run."

"Sure. That was a computer running at top efficiency. Obviously the Boogeyman program clogged up the computer somehow."

"Obviously," said Counselor Troi.

"Obviously," said Dr. Crusher.

"So the captain called a meeting of the crew on the recreation deck of the simulated *Enterprise.* When enough of them had arrived, there was a big flash and the whole simulation disappeared."

"A remarkable story," Troi said. "You really are a hero."

"Not me," said Wesley. "Data's the hero. Captain Picard's the hero."

"Neither of them was forced to confront his childhood fears." Troi watched Wesley very seriously.

"Absolutely," Dr. Crusher said.

"Yeah, well, if I hadn't designed them that way, I wouldn't have had to confront them that way."

They drank for a while. Wesley looked out the window at the rainbows. They were still creeping along at warp five so that Shubunkin would have time to debrief Baldwin before the *Enterprise* reached Memory Alpha. Thinking about the shuddering turbolift and the blue plastic spaceship made Wesley uneasy, but he could not stop himself. He'd have to see Geordi and Data as soon as he could.

"So," said Dr. Crusher, "did you find out what you wanted to know?"

"What do you mean?"

"You went to the holodeck to test yourself in a command situation. How did you do?"

"Mom, I got snookered by my own program."

"This time."

That stopped Wesley. He'd gotten so bound up in feeling sorry for himself, because of the trouble caused by his Boogeyman program, because he'd lost his ship during the *Kobayashi Maru* incident, that it hadn't occurred to him that he might get a second chance.

Speaking out loud but to himself, Wesley said, "I'll write a new, improved Boogeyman program, one without the bugs."

"Experience is a great teacher," Troi said.

Wesley's head exploded with theories, equations, possibilities. He found it difficult to stay in his chair. He needed to talk with Data and Geordi right now.

"You did good, kid," Dr. Crusher said and poked him in the shoulder.

"Yeah," said Wesley and smiled.

Picard visited the bridge and discovered to his relief that the computer malfunction was limited to the holodeck. Riker said, "Still cruising at warp five. All readings nominal."

"Anything from Starfleet on Commander Mont?"

"Evidently Commander Mont visited Axer a year ago on a diplomatic mission. Starfleet security suspects that the man who came back was this assassin."

"But certainly, keeping up the charade would have been difficult. He would have needed to submit to computer verification occasionally."

"Evidently," Riker said, "he was clever enough to maneuver others to be verified. He got in on their say-so."

Picard nodded. "Other moles?"

"None have turned up yet, sir."

"Unfortunately, a negative result, though possibly correct, is never satisfying."

"You always wonder what you missed."

"Indeed." The captain wondered if more of Professor Baldwin's enemies awaited him. A negative result would certainly not be satisfying to him. Paranoia thrived on negative results. Picard said, "Very well, Number One. I'll be with Shubunkin and Baldwin in the exobiology lab on deck five." He made as if to leave.

"Oh, and Captain, good to have you back."

"That's what was odd about my little adventure. I was never actually away." Picard shook his head. The *Enterprise* was his home. Having it turn against him was not something he would care to experience again.

"I'd be interested in hearing about it, if you'd like to talk."

Would I? Picard wondered. He was generally a very private person, but the impulse to share one's experiences was strong in humans, as it was in many races; the feeling was working hard in Picard at the moment. Troi would probably say that he needed to talk out his ambivalent feelings about the holodeck, but as far as Picard was concerned, he was just telling a good story.

"Indeed I would, Number One." He sat down in the command chair and ruminated while Riker sat down next to him. Except for the normal twitters and chirps—the sound of the ship talking to itself—the bridge was silent. Ensign Winston-Smyth was at the conn and Ensign Perry was at Ops, standing by in the unlikely event the main computer needed a human backup. Stars—their appearance having been corrected by the viewscreen—looked normal as they poured toward the *Enterprise*, despite the ship's warp speed.

As Picard spoke in his clear, clipped voice, he noticed Winston-Smyth and Perry cocking their heads a little, listening without being obvious about it. The captain didn't mind. What had happened on the holodeck was not a secret and, in fact, might prove instructive to others. Word would get around the ship. Of course, word would get around anyway. Scuttlebutt was still the fastest thing in Starfleet, not excepting galaxy-class starships.

Wesley finally escaped from Counselor Troi and his mom and went down to Engineering. He found Geordi and Data at a work station watching the readout screen flash as the holodeck satellite of the main computer ran a processor diagnostic on itself.

"Anything?" said Wesley.

While still watching the screen, Data said, "The Boogeyman program is gone, overwritten when the computer drew on more memory to fill the recreation deck with crew members."

"No significant abnormalities," La Forge said, and touched a control surface. The display froze, and he ran his finger under a line of code. He touched the control again, and the screen began to serve up more information.

"I thought everything was significant," Wesley said.

La Forge shook his head. "A starship is the most complicated piece of machinery ever built by any of the Federation races. Its programs are enormously complicated, too, and the main computer and its satellites talk to one another all the time. Code gets duplicated. Information is recorded someplace where it might never be needed again. Subroutines written for specific one-shot purposes are left in memory. Every year or so we have to go into the computer with a machete and clear out the underbrush."

Data looked horrified. "I presume you are speaking metaphorically."

"More or less," La Forge said.

The computer said, "End of diagnostic. No significant abnormalities."

"That's a relief," Wesley said, thinking about the turbolift and the blue plastic spaceship.

La Forge turned his head in Wesley's direction and said, "Yeah, it is. But you're relieved about more than just the lack of abnormalities."

"Maybe." Wesley told them about the two abnormalities he'd just observed. "Significant or not?" he asked.

"I'd say not," La Forge said. "According to the diagnostic, the Boogeymen are gone. Right, Data?"

"So it would seem."

La Forge shook his head and said, "I don't know why I allow pessimists in Engineering." He raised his voice and said, "Computer, start machete program."

Data glanced at him in surprise.

"Running," the computer said.

"If you haven't found anything," Wesley said, "the problem must have been with the Boogeyman program itself."

"I don't see any other answer," La Forge said.

"And yet," Data said in the reasonable voice Wesley sometimes found maddening, "the Boogeyman program had nothing in it that might cause such a malfunction."

"You remember the entire program?" La Forge said.

"Of course. An android never forgets."

"I've heard a lot about that Boogeyman program," La Forge said. "Hell, I'm the one who installed it in the holodeck. I'd like to take a look at it."

"I can type it out in just a few minutes," Data said. He sat down at an empty work station and began to type so fast his fingers were a blur.

"I'd like to try it again," Wesley said.

"What? The Boogeymen? The training program?"

"Both," said Wesley.

Even with his eyes covered, La Forge gave the impression he was squinting at Wesley. He said, "You'd better let me take a look at the programs first, Wes. Data doesn't make mistakes, but sometimes even correct code can do funny things inside a starship mainframe."

Riker had listened to Picard's story with some amazement. Though he'd used the Starfleet training programs just as every other fleet officer had, Riker claimed that he always knew in his gut when he was inside a holodeck simulation and when he was experiencing something real. "It must have been like a nightmare," he said of Picard's experience. "You never knew if you were really awake or just dreaming you were awake."

Riker's comment struck Picard hard. He smiled. "Of course, Number One. You are referring to the philosophical conundrum stated by Chuang-tzu."

Riker looked uncomfortable, the way he always did when Picard sprang a history lesson on him. "Vulcan?" Riker asked hopefully.

Picard shook his head. "You must read your history, Number One. Chuang-tzu was not Vulcan but a philosopher of ancient Earth, fourth century B.C. China, to be exact. On awakening from a dream he wondered if he had been a man dreaming he was a butterfly, or was now a butterfly dreaming he was a man."

"Ah," said Riker.

"Ah, indeed." Picard ordered Riker to carry on and left for the exobiology lab, grumbling to himself yet again that Starfleet Academy was perhaps a little light on the humanities.

He nodded to the security guard stationed outside the laboratory door and entered. Shubunkin and

Baldwin were contemplating a model of the teardrop ship. Baldwin pointed a clear wand at the ship, and the top became transparent. He touched one of the miniature chairs with the wand and made it rise a few inches above the model.

"If we can believe these chairs," Baldwin said, "the members of the crew looked like us; they bent the way we do, anyway."

"That confirms the sensor readings we recorded on our first contact. Nintey-eight percent human. But humans need instrumentality. There's no indication that they were telekinetic."

Almost to himself, Picard said, "And yet they attained warp speed without warp engines."

"Yes, yes," Shubunkin said irritably. "Actually we have found instrumentation of a sort." He took the wand from Baldwin and pointed to an artifact near the tail of the ship that looked like nothing so much as a small bass drum. "As near as we can determine, this focuses some kind of energy."

"What kind?"

Baldwin shook his head, but he was not disagreeing with Shubunkin. He looked whipped. "Power output curves show a connection between the focusing mechanism and humanoid brain activity. Where that leads, who knows?"

The three of them stared at the teardrop. Evidently d'Ort'd technology was so different from anything in the Federation that none of the usual signposts were helpful. Picard said, "Sensors indicated the humanoids were asleep while the ship was in flight. If, for the sake of argument, we assume that the humanoid brain activity has something to do with the ship moving at warp speeds, perhaps the sleeping does, too?"

Shubunkin glanced at Baldwin to see what effect Picard's question had had. Baldwin shrugged.

"We're still missing something," Shubunkin said. "Some essential part of the puzzle."

"What about the natives of Tantamon Four?" Picard said.

"According to Baldwin's diaries," Shubunkin said, "the natives cannot be the builders."

"Perhaps their ancestors?" Picard said.

"Degenerate descendants?" Shubunkin said. "Impossible. Baldwin found no advanced artifacts except this single ship. Correct?"

"Correct," Baldwin said, and made talking-mouth motions with one hand as he rolled his eyes.

Shubunkin pointedly ignored Baldwin's impolite gestures and said, "Professor Baldwin's own observations support the fact that the natives advance by cooperating instead of by competing, the method used by the natives of Earth and so many other planets. I've found evidence of competition on the ship."

"Your evidence is based on a theory."

"It is a law of exology!"

"It's a theory developed by a bunch of guys who've never been in the field!"

"Gentlemen, please," Picard shouted to be heard over their argument.

Quietly, sarcastically, Shubunkin said, "Professor Baldwin has a theory of his own." It was a dare.

"It's in the ship's software," Baldwin said, a little angrily, as if he'd suggested this before to no effect.

Shubunkin said, "Can you understand the software? I can't. I'm no computer expert. And even if you claim to understand it, you can still be wrong. We need primary data."

"Software is a tool. It has its own logic. I understand it well enough. I don't know why you get so defensive when I suggest that the humanoid d'Ort'd are the servants of the other, more alien species."

"A servant, like their ship," Shubunkin said sarcastically. "What does that mean? I tell you we need a second opinion."

"One of your would-be exologists?"

It was obvious to Picard that these two had for hours been daring each other to cross a line and that neither of them was going to budge. He said, "Perhaps Mr. Data can be of help. Few beings know more about computers and their software than he."

Baldwin said, "Sounds good to me."

Shubunkin shrugged and folded his arms.

Picard tapped his insignia and said, "Mr. Data."

"Here, Captain."

"Would you please join me in the exobiology lab on deck five?"

"On my way, sir."

Data arrived, the usual inquisitive expression on his face. Baldwin said, "Maybe now we can get somewhere, eh, Data?"

Data looked puzzled. "Have we met, sir?"

A cold wind blew through Picard. He shot Data a look and said with exaggerated care, "This is Professor Baldwin. We picked him up on Tantamon Four. You escorted him to the conference lounge."

"I did?" Data said.

"You did," said Picard. Baldwin and Shubunkin looked at him, mystified.

"Something wrong, Captain?" Shubunkin said.

"As you may have known, Data is an android. To my knowledge he's never before forgotten anything."

"It did?" Data said.

"You did," said Picard. Thelwren and Shubunkin looked at him, surprised.

"Something wrong, Captain?" Shubunkin said.

"As you know how Data is, 'Data is so critical. To my complexity before it became fragmented . . ."

Chapter Eight

DATA SAID, "I am incapable of forgetting anything." He noted the worried expression on Picard's face. "Have I forgotten something, sir?"

"It would seem so."

"Forgetfulness is a most interesting sensation," said Data. He stood motionless, a half smile on his face.

Picard had seen Data like this before. Riker had once called him Pinocchio, and that appellation was not far from the truth. Data was fascinated with humans and humanity. Picard feared that instead of being dismayed by his defect, Data was intrigued by it.

"Lieutenant Commander," Picard said in a purposely harsh voice.

Data looked at him. "Yes, sir?"

More kindly, Picard said, "Given your recent linking with the main computer of the holodeck *Enter-*

prise, I am concerned that your memory failure may be a symptom of more serious matters."

"It is certainly possible, sir."

"I suggest you run a diagnostic program on yourself immediately."

"Ah. Might I suggest, sir, that by your same reasoning, my internal diagnostic programs are not to be trusted. As indeed, I am not."

Worse and worse, Picard thought. What did Data expect Picard to do, throw him in the brig? Picard was distressed to find that he considered this a real option. Hoping for something better, he said, "What do you suggest?"

"It is not likely that the main computer has been contaminated by the Boogeymen. Therefore, I suggest that I allow the main computer to diagnose me. I suggest further that you ask Mr. La Forge to supervise this procedure."

"Done." He tapped his insignia and said, "Mr. La Forge."

"Here, Captain."

"Meet me in the computer center on deck ten immediately."

"On my way."

Baldwin and Shubunkin did not entirely appreciate the seriousness of Picard's problem, but they took time out from their quarrel and wished him well.

Picard and Data hurried to deck ten, and Picard went through the identification process that had not worked for him on the holo-*Enterprise.* As the doors to the computer core control center slid open, La Forge arrived with Wesley. Picard glanced at Wesley but did not object to his presence. He might have something valuable to offer.

The doors closed behind them, and they were alone with the main access to the brain of *Enterprise*. La Forge walked to the situation wall and studied it for a moment. "Everything seems normal, sir. What's the problem?"

"It's Mr. Data. He's forgotten Professor Baldwin." Wesley started to speak, then thought better of it.

La Forge raised his eyebrows and nodded. He said, "You'll want a full diagnostic on him. Come on over here, Data. This won't hurt a bit."

"I didn't expect that it would," Data said as he crossed to the wall of electronic ports. La Forge used an optical cable to plug him in, then sat down at one of the four central terminals and brought it up. Picard and Wesley backed off, watching as if La Forge and Data were performers in a stage play.

"Put yourself into passive mode," La Forge said as he made adjustments on his board.

"Done," said Data in a strange, flat voice.

La Forge said, "We don't have enough room in the mainframe for all Data's programming, but we do have a copy of his diagnostic program, just in case something like this should come up." He set a few defaults and said, "Just relax. Computer."

"Working," said the computer voice and Data at the same time.

"Access and run diagnostic program 'Data' on peripheral in port 6-665A."

"Working," Data and the computer said together.

Picard didn't know what he expected to see, but what he did see was nothing. The computer spoke to itself in staccato electronic tones while La Forge sat back with his arms folded, watching Data. The android did not move. The expression on his face was blank. Picard said, "Anything to report on the holodeck problem, Mr. La Forge?"

"Nothing yet, sir. But I have a few more things to check."

Picard nodded. He was eager to find out what the problem was. A few days or even weeks without the holodeck would probably not have a significant effect on his crew, but as Counselor Troi was certain to remind him, the ability to use the holodeck was important to their mental health. And La Forge knew what he was doing.

The computer stopped twittering, and Data frowned.

"Data?" La Forge said.

Data worked the cable clear at either end and replaced his scalp. He rubbed his forehead with one hand while he stumbled to a chair and nearly fell into it.

"Data?" they all said as they converged on him.

"I feel most unusual," Data said.

"Unusual, how?" Picard said.

Data's mouth moved without making a sound. He seemed to be gathering his thoughts. Picard knew that Data occasionally had to access information from a nether part of his positronic brain, but he never had to organize his thoughts, at least not the way natural life forms did. Data's thoughts *arrived* organized.

Wesley said, "If I looked like that, Mom would have me down in sickbay. And I'd probably go."

"Data?" Picard said.

"Most unusual," Data said again. "My head and limbs are throbbing in a most unpleasant way. I feel very weak and tired."

"Are you sick, Data?" La Forge said.

"Sick? Accessing." Data made the usual jerky reading motions with his head. He stopped suddenly, a pained look on his face and a hand to his temple. He said, "Sick. Ill. Ailing. Disabled. Not up to snuff. I have no way of knowing if this describes my condition, never having felt this way before. But it is a logical working hypothesis. I do seem to be not up to snuff." He smiled, evidently felt pain, and touched his temple again. "Captain, may I be excused?"

"If you were any other crew member, I'd send you to sickbay. What do you suggest, Mr. La Forge?"

"It *does* seem to be an engineering problem. And though I'm not a doctor, I doubt if what he has is contagious to other members of the crew. Come on down to Engineering, Data."

"Very well. This is most interesting. Ow."

"Ensign Crusher, would you see that Mr. Data arrives in Engineering safely."

"Aye, sir."

They got Data to his feet, and he and Wesley shuffled out together.

When the door had closed, Picard said, "It seems likely that Data was infected by the main computer."

"It seems that way."

"Is this related somehow to our holodeck problem?"

"You better hope not, sir. If we have Boogeymen in our mainframe, we are in big trouble."

"Exactly how big?"

"I don't know at the moment. But Data being sick could be a break for us."

"How so?"

"It gives us two views of the problem rather than just one. The parallax could give us a clue or two."

"I want some answers, Mr. La Forge. Or at the very least, better questions. One hour in the conference lounge."

"Aye, sir," said La Forge as he quickly left the room.

Picard looked around. In the entire Federation only three or four cases of mental illness were reported every year. Not one case of computer mental illness had been reported in many years. If the mainframe of the *Enterprise* was the statistical anomaly, Picard was not confident that La Forge's ideas about parallax would save them.

Down in Engineering Wesley deposited Data in a chair, then sat across from him and watched. It was odd to see Data, who never got tired and normally had the posture of a machine, with his elbows on the table, slumping. He touched his forehead and winced occasionally. Yet Data's skin color was the same as it always was and he didn't sweat. Wesley guessed that he probably didn't have a temperature. He had an operating temperature, but that wasn't the same thing.

Wesley said, "How do you feel?"

Data looked puzzled for a moment and then said, "Generally, with my hands, but I have sensors all over my body. Did I say something funny, Wesley?"

Wesley shook his head and said, "Sometimes I think that pretending you don't know what humor is is the funniest thing about you."

Data didn't understand that, and Wesley knew it was pointless to try explaining it, so he just forged on with another question. He said, "What is your condition?"

"Much the same as it was before. Tell me about being sick."

Wesley considered the question. Most ailments that were common before the twenty-third century had been eradicated. Still, germs, viruses, and other afflictions mutated constantly and were sometimes accidentally carried from one outpost of the Federation to another. People even occasionally caught cold. Wesley suspected that Data knew all this and really wanted to know how humans reacted to being sick. Data was a great one for playacting. His rendition of Sherlock Holmes was not the end. The drama group he directed was famous all over the ship.

Wesley said, "I had a cold once."

"Cold? As in heatless, chilly, nippy, frigid—"

"No, Data. A cold. A viral infection causing you to sneeze and cough and have a fever. Nothing really hurts, but you get bored with sneezing and coughing, and that's after the infection makes you tired to begin with."

"I see that being the son of a doctor has had its effect on you."

Wesley was pleased by that, but he said, "Everybody knows this stuff, Data. But the important part as far as you're concerned, is that when you have a cold you lie in bed with tissues to sneeze into and all your favorite books and a portable computer terminal and maybe some games you can play by yourself and a glass of water and some cough drops."

"Sounds cluttered."

"Maybe if you were well it would be, but if you're sick, it's just comfortable."

"I see. Comfort is a consideration."

Wesley nodded.

"Useful information. Please excuse me," Data said and rested his head on his crossed arms.

Wesley sat there feeling helpless. If Data were human, he'd already be in sickbay. If he were just a machine, Wesley would already be poking a hyperspanner around inside him. But Data was supposed to be self-adjusting. He wasn't supposed to get sick or broken or whatever.

When La Forge emerged from the turbolift, Wesley went over to talk to him.

"How is he?" La Forge said.

"Not so good. But he's having fun with it."

"That's our Data."

They watched Data for a while. He wasn't moving. Which in Data's case meant nothing. Wesley said, "Did he catch this from the mainframe?"

"I hope not, but the evidence is pretty clear, isn't it?"

"Yeah. Does this have anything to do with my Boogeymen?"

"The diagnostics didn't find the program. But even if the Boogeyman program somehow got through, the machete program would have cleaned it out."

"That's a relief."

"You may be relieved, my boy," La Forge said as he

put an arm around Wesley's shoulders and guided him toward Data, "but personally, I'd rather have Boogeymen. At least I'd know what the problem was and how to deal with it. As things are . . ." He shrugged.

Data looked up as they approached and attempted to erect a smile. La Forge said, "Can I plug you in again, Data? I'd like to run a little diagnostic of my own."

"Of course," Data said. "Just what the doctor ordered."

"How about some hot chocolate?" Wesley said.

"I must remind you, Wesley, that I do not eat."

"I know that. But I've seen you mimic eating for social occasions. I just thought a cup of hot chocolate would make you feel better."

"This is part of being sick?"

"If you're lucky," La Forge said.

"Very well."

Wesley went to a food slot and said, "Hot chocolate in a cup. With a marshmallow." He grinned at Data.

"Very plush," La Forge said.

However, what came from the slot was not a steaming cup but a large platter with a red spiderlike creature lying in the center surrounded by greens and lemon wedges. Something round, soft, and purple was caught between its jaws.

"Geordi," Wesley said, very worried.

La Forge came over to look at what had come from the food slot. "Denebian Slime Devil à la Tellarite," he said.

"Yeah, but I asked for hot chocolate."

Another cooked slime devil appeared on the stage,

knocking the first one to the floor. And then another after that.

"Computer," La Forge called out.

"Working," the computer said.

Wesley stared at the slot in horror.

"What the hell kind of computer voice was that?" La Forge said.

Wesley swallowed and said, "That was the voice of a Boogeyman."

They watched the food slot produce another plate of Denebian Slime Devil à la Tellarite. La Forge ran for the master situation monitor while he called for his staff.

Chapter Nine

THE MOOD IN the conference lounge was glum, and Picard saw no reason to lighten it. For the tenth time since sitting down at the head of the table, he punched the ready button on his memo terminal. The Starfleet logo faded from the screen and was replaced by the word "Working." Picard said, "Report status of *Enterprise* systems." On the screen the words "One moment please" appeared, and then gibberish rolled across it. Picard was not surprised. He'd gotten gibberish the other nine times, too. Gibberish was the language of the day all over the ship. "Cancel," Picard said. The computer worked to the extent that the screen went blank and the Starfleet logo came up again.

Picard looked around at his senior officers and said, "Mr. La Forge, what is Mr. Data's condition?"

"He seems to be suffering from a minor breakdown of all his systems. His efficiency is down twenty-two percent, his operating temperature is up four degrees Celsius. The activity in his positronic brain is erratic, but my training is in propulsion and ships systems. If I could fix him, I'd be Dr. Soong, but I'm not."

"Can he repair himself?"

"Data seems convinced that he can. His maintenance programs act like our white blood cells; they seek out enemy code and destroy it. Assuming, of course, that his maintenance programs have been designed to fight this particular enemy."

"Is there a chance they haven't?"

"It's a big universe, sir."

Picard knew that La Forge was right. He nodded philosophically and said, "Dr. Crusher, do you have an opinion?"

Dr. Crusher shrugged and made a motion of dismissal. She said, "Data's an android and even further outside my specialty than he is outside Lieutenant Commander La Forge's. But I've given him every test that seems relevant. If he were human, I'd say he had the flu."

"Flu?" Riker said.

"Influenza. A group of very contagious viruses that ran rampant through human history. Sometimes the sickness caused by a virus was no worse than a bad cold. But it could kill, too." Dr. Crusher smiled. "Some early virologists called a virus bad news wrapped in protein."

Riker said, "How is Data's problem related to our computer problem?"

La Forge spoke with his hands as well as his mouth. For him, problems had shapes and sizes. He said, "It's pretty obvious that Data was contaminated when he plugged into the ship's computer to run a diagnostic. I'd say that whatever has Data down is also the cause of the problem we have with the ship's computer."

Riker said, "Then if Data's maintenance programs are able to cure him, all we have to do is load those programs into the ship's computer."

"It might work," La Forge allowed, "but we'd be taking quite a chance. First, Data's maintenance programs were designed just for him and his positronic brain. They probably won't work inside the ship's computer. Catching the flu is easy. Curing it is a much more sophisticated operation. Second, if we plug Data into the ship's computer again, he might pick up another dose of whatever it is. Next time it might be fatal."

Picard slapped the table and said, "I hope we never become desperate enough to test Mr. La Forge's theories. The fact that none of you seems to have noticed is that Mr. Data was infected twice."

"Sir?" La Forge said.

Picard realized that he and Wesley were the only ones at the table who had observed Data both plugging into the holo-computer and then into the real computer. He shared that information with the others.

Surprised, Wesley said, "Of course. Data had forgotten Professor Baldwin before Geordi ran the diagnostic on him. That's *why* we ran the diagnostic on him."

Riker said, "Data's second infection seems to have a different effect on him than his first."

"Another clue, Mr. La Forge?" Picard said.

La Forge thought for a moment before he admitted that it probably was. "But at this point I don't even have a good guess as to what it tells us."

Picard had confidence that La Forge would find the solution, with or without the help of Wesley and Data. But they couldn't brood about it now. Picard went on with the air of a man changing the subject. "This sounds similar to the problem we and the *Yamato* had with the program broadcast by the Iconian probe. Can we just turn off the ship and restart, using protected master programs?"

Mention of the *Yamato* made everybody thoughtful. The *Yamato* had been the *Enterprise*'s sister ship. It was her destruction that had given La Forge the clue he needed to save the *Enterprise*.

La Forge looked uncomfortable. He lifted his open hand and tilted it from side to side. "I don't think so, sir. This time the core itself seems to be blocked."

Wesley said, "Not just protected?"

"Sure. The main core is protected by shields, triple redundant circuits, debugging programs, and some things so secret that Starfleet tells you about them only if you have a need to know. But now, it's been entirely cut off. The satellite computers that are normally coordinated by the core are now running the ship themselves. I don't know how—but as I said before, it's a big universe."

Riker said, "You think we've run into something the Starfleet engineers didn't think of?"

La Forge shrugged. "Looks that way, sir."

The room was silent again. Wesley began to squirm, and at last words were squeezed out of him. He said,

"The Boogeymen caused all this trouble?" He looked even more uncomfortable than La Forge.

"Not all by themselves, Wes. The diagnostics didn't find the Boogeyman program. But even if it somehow got through undetected, the machete program would have cleaned it out by now."

Wesley nodded. He seemed relieved.

Dr. Crusher said, "Then the Boogeyman program must be working along with some other program."

La Forge said, "You were talking about viruses before, Doctor. That's what we have."

Picard remembered that the Iconian program had been a computer virus, too. Only by shutting down every *Enterprise* system and then reloading every program had they saved the ship. "Continue, Mr. La Forge."

La Forge stood up and called into operation a screen at the end of the conference lounge.

"It works," Wesley said with some surprise.

"Yeah," said La Forge. "So far. Computer, exhibit 'Virus.'"

"Working," said the computer. It sounded like a Boogeyman. Picard saw Wesley shudder.

The screen rolled a few times, and when the picture steadied, it was a schematic of *Enterprise*'s computer system. La Forge said, "This is basically a smaller, simplified version of the flow chart in the main computer center. If everything were working properly, this chart would update itself automatically as the situation changed. But what you're looking at is not connected to the computer. It is a picture of the situation as it was twenty minutes ago." He pointed out specific areas. "Normal information flow is in gold. Satellites of the computer brain afflicted by the virus are in red."

"Almost half," Riker said.

"Forty-seven percent," La Forge said.

"Twenty minutes ago," Picard said. Forty-seven percent. Fifty-two. Seventy-three. When would the ship become unlivable? How long before navigation and life support went down? He said, "How long do we have till we can no longer function, even at the most basic level?"

"Impossible to say, sir. The virus is spreading by fits and starts, as a clean satellite calls on information in a contaminated part. Could be hours or days. Certainly no more than a week, and that's only if we are very lucky."

"We'll shut down all nonessential systems," said Riker.

"Yes," said Picard, "and then only essential systems will become infected." There had to be a loose thread, a way out. "Number One, alert all passengers and crew to use the greatest discretion when accessing the computer. Use it as if it were a natural resource that was running dry. Also, for the duration we are shutting down all recreational functions."

"Aye, Captain." They waited while Riker called the bridge and repeated the captain's instructions into his communicator. Mr. Worf acknowledged.

When Riker was done, Picard said, "How did the Boogeyman program get into the system?"

La Forge sat down, the energy he had shown during his presentation suddenly gone. He said, "My theory, sir, is that when it spread to the holodeck computer, somehow the virus and the Boogeymen got hooked together."

Riker said, "And then the virus program hauled the Boogeymen everywhere it went."

"That's the way I see it." La Forge was almost apologizing.

Picard thought about what La Forge had just said. It was all very neat. All very logical. It was probably correct as well. "This is my doing, then," he said.

"Well, sir—"

"When I forced the Boogeyman program to disappear, it was not overwritten, as Mr. Data and I thought. It simply went somewhere else."

Dr. Crusher moved as if to put her hand on Picard's, but took it back without touching him. She said, "You didn't know, sir."

"Mr. Crusher didn't know. I didn't know." He shook his head and then smiled as if he had just begun to understand some cosmic joke. "Overloading the computer seemed like a good idea at the time. Which is the best defense any of us can ever give when caught making a mistake of this magnitude."

"We have to answer two questions, then," Riker said. "First, where did the virus program come from? And second, how do we get rid of the virus-Boogeyman combination?"

Good old Riker, trying to distract him from blaming himself for something no one could have known.

"I have a theory about the first question, too," La Forge said, sounding somewhat embarrassed. He'd had a difficult day, Picard thought. First accusing his captain of scuttling his own ship—if only accidentally

—and now accusing one of the captain's friends of helping the process along.

"Go on, Mr. La Forge," Picard said, smiling his most encouraging smile.

La Forge said, "I think we can take it as given that Data has the same virus as the satellite computer system; he was infected when he plugged in to be diagnosed."

Everyone nodded.

"And after the flu symptoms, what is the most obvious characteristic of Data's condition?"

"He's forgotten Professor Baldwin," Wesley said.

"But," Dr. Crusher said, "that happened when he plugged into the holo-computer—which the Boogeymen controlled."

"Right," said La Forge, "but I believe the two events are connected."

"How?" said Picard.

"Okay," said La Forge, molding the explanation in the air. "Imagine we have these two programs. At the time Data plugged into the holo-computer, he was contaminated by the virus, which caused him to forget Professor Baldwin."

Dr. Crusher did not look happy, but she nodded along with everyone else.

"Now, as the virus spread through the system, it dragged the Boogeyman program along with it. The Boogeyman program, being more aggressive than the virus, reproduced itself faster, became stronger, and was able to afflict Data with something that looks like the flu."

"Let me see if I have this straight," Dr. Crusher said. "Wesley programs the holodeck computer with

Boogeymen. Somebody infects the computer system with a virus that erases references to Professor Baldwin. When it infects the holodeck computer, the virus somehow gets connected with the Boogeyman program."

"Right so far," La Forge said.

"When the captain distracted the holodeck computer by filling the recreation deck with holo-people, the Boogeyman-virus combination was squeezed into the system, and from there it was able to spread."

"Right again."

"All of which means what?" Dr. Crusher said.

Riker smiled in appreciation. "You don't have a devious enough mind, Doctor. If all reference to Professor Baldwin has been erased, the chances are good that he is the one who designed the virus."

La Forge, having recovered most of his equilibrium, said, "You see what I mean about parallax, Captain? Data's problems give us insight into the ship's problems."

"Mont can't be Professor Baldwin's only enemy," Dr. Crusher said. "Maybe they're trying to make Baldwin a nonperson, discredit him that way."

"No, Doctor," said Picard. "I believe that Commander Riker is correct."

"For what reason?" Dr. Crusher asked.

The answer was obvious to Picard. Particularly given Baldwin's private comments about wanting, needing, to disappear. In an information-intensive society such as the Federation, the place to start would be with the records. How better to proceed than by using a computer virus designed to wipe out every mention of his name, every bit of evidence he ever existed? Picard did not feel free to mention any of this, not even now. But he would have to speak with Eric Baldwin very soon.

Picard said, "Something Professor Baldwin said to me. Mr. La Forge, why didn't your diagnostic program find Baldwin's virus when it searched the computer? More important, why didn't the machete program clear it?"

"When we find that out," La Forge said, "we'll know how to get rid of the virus. I say we start finding out by talking to Professor Baldwin."

Riker touched his insignia and said, "Lieutenant Worf."

"Here, Commander." Worf's voice pierced the room like a steel shaft.

"Bring Professor Baldwin to the conference lounge on deck one."

"Belay that order, Mr. Worf."

"Aye, Captain," Worf said, sounding a little confused.

Riker's eyebrows were up, which meant the captain had surprised him. Picard had almost succeeded in surprising himself. He said, "I'll speak to him first."

"Very well, sir," Riker said in a tone that meant he was willing to go along with Picard, for the moment anyway. One of the things that made Riker valuable was that he knew when to disagree with his superior officer. Picard knew that time would come soon. But Riker trusted him and would allow him some rope.

When Picard stood up, the others did as well. He said, "Mr. La Forge, I want you and Mr. Data to track down, analyze, and counteract the Boogeyman-virus combination. Minimal use of the computer, if you please."

La Forge nodded and said, "We'll use tricorders." He strode out.

"The rest of you stay alert," Picard said. "If you have any ideas, even if they seem ridiculous, please see Mr. La Forge. This situation does not seem to welcome conservative thinking."

Dr. Crusher and Commander Riker followed La Forge onto the bridge. When the doors closed, Picard said, "What is it, Mr. Crusher?"

"I'm sorry, Captain."

"For what?"

"For the Boogeymen. For the mess we're in now."

"It seems that we've both made a number of mistakes."

"Yes, sir."

"You are determined to take this all on your own shoulders."

"Well, yes, sir. If it hadn't been for the Boogeymen—"

Picard sighed and said, "Mr. Crusher, I would like to quote a poem to you."

"Yes, sir," Wesley said, bewildered.

Picard recited:

> "Once in a stately passion
> I cried with desperate grief,
> 'O Lord, my heart is black with guile,
> Of sinners I am chief.'

Then stooped my guardian angel
And whispered from behind,
'Vanity, my little man,
You're nothing of the kind.'

"Do you understand, Wesley? It is sometimes arrogant to claim *all* the guilt."

Picard caught Wesley trying not to smile and said, "Go. Try to stay out of trouble."

"Yes, sir."

Wesley went out, leaving Picard to ponder his own arrogance. He sighed again and left the conference lounge.

In Engineering, La Forge discovered that Data had gone to his cabin. La Forge took the turbolift back up and pushed the announce button outside Data's door.

Data said, "Cub in."

"Cub in?" La Forge said as he entered. He found Data sitting at his desk surrounded by an incredible array of stuff: stacks of bound books, a game generator with a number of game chips, a box of tissues. Nearby was a cup of room-temperature brown liquid with a foamy white island floating on the surface—hot chocolate with a marshmallow. In Data's mouth was a glass tube no larger than a pencil, and on top of his head was a sack that sat there like a small lumpy mountain. He was dressed in a blue robe held closed by a golden cord.

"Data, what is all this?"

Data was about to answer when he inhaled convulsively. With one hand he pulled the glass tube from his mouth and with the other he grabbed a tissue. "Ah-ah-

ah-choo!" He sneezed into the tissue, and the bag slid off his head and onto the floor, where it disgorged ice cubes and cold water.

"Dis is a terbobedder," Data said, holding up the glass tube. "And dis is tissue for wed I sneeze."

"You sound all stuffy."

"Ob course. I hab a code in by dose."

La Forge shook his head in disbelief. "You can't have a cold, Data. You're an android."

"I ab exploring de human condition 'do be sick.'"

"You can explore that later. The captain wants us to get busy on that computer virus."

Data stood and dramatically threw off the robe. Underneath was his uniform. He said, "I believe I have contrived some theories on how we might proceed." Magically, his nose was no longer stuffy.

"You must be feeling better."

"I must," said Data agreeably.

He and La Forge walked out into the corridor, spouting computer science at each other enthusiastically.

Picard sat behind the desk in his ready room glaring at his memo terminal, wondering if asking it a question was worth the frustration of not getting an answer. He'd already called Professor Baldwin in the exobiology lab and requested his presence. He could have sent Worf or some other member of the security team to escort him, but Picard preferred not to do that. Even if Baldwin had in fact loaded the virus into the *Enterprise*'s computer, he was not likely to be violent. It was just as well that sending somebody to get Baldwin had turned out not to be necessary.

"Somebody's at the door," a Boogeyman voice called. The voice startled Picard. Only moments before, when Riker had looked in on him with a routine matter, the door had made its usual audio twinkle. Wesley's Boogeymen were taking over the ship. Something had to be done, and soon.

"Come," Picard called.

The door slid open and Baldwin walked in, looking a little sheepish. He said, "That sounds like your official captain-type voice."

"I'm afraid it is, Eric. Please sit down."

Baldwin sat in the chair across from Picard, lifted an ankle across a knee, and rested his hands in his lap. Picard contemplated him, trying to decide where to begin. He noticed Baldwin contemplating *him* and couldn't help smiling. He said, "You've heard that the ship is running at less than its usual efficiency."

"Shubunkin and I heard the announcement about not using the computer." Baldwin shook his head. "Unfortunately this was immediately after I'd asked a food slot for a cup of coffee."

"What happened?"

"I got something brown and hot in a cup. It had no smell. I tried a little. It was like swallowing my own spit."

"Must you be so graphic?"

"Trained observer. Sorry. What about the computer?"

Picard straightened his tunic and said, "The mainframe of the *Enterprise* computer has been attacked by a virus. It seems that one of the things this virus is designed to do is eradicate any mention of your existence."

Baldwin shook his head and said, "I have a lot of enemies, Jean-Luc. Some of them are pretty damned clever. One of them wants to make trouble for me. I'm sorry."

"You expect me to believe that after all you told me about wanting to disappear? You know you're pretty damned clever yourself."

Baldwin continued to look at him as if he hadn't heard a word Picard said.

"Eric?" Picard said.

Baldwin slumped over in his chair.

Picard was just rising to see if Professor Baldwin was all right when Riker's voice came over the comlink. "Captain Picard to the bridge, please."

Picard touched a companel and said, "Dr. Crusher to the captain's ready room."

"We're a little busy right now, Captain."

The door to the ready room opened and Riker came in, looking very worried indeed. "Captain?"

"I'll be right there, Number One. Dr. Crusher, send someone as quickly as you can. Professor Baldwin has apparently fainted."

As Picard walked out onto the bridge, he said, "What is it, Number One?" Then he saw Dr. Crusher bending over Counselor Troi. Worf stood nearby, alert, ready for anything, one hand on his ceremonial dagger.

"She fainted," Riker said.

"She's all right for the moment," Dr. Crusher said, "but I should get her to sickbay." An orderly gently maneuvered Troi onto a null-grav stretcher and carried her away.

"What about Baldwin?" Picard said.

Dr. Crusher nodded and hurried across the bridge to the ready room.

"That's not all, Captain," Riker said. "We're cruising at warp eight."

"Who gave the order?" Picard said as he sat down in his command chair.

"No one, sir. And we can't stop."

Picard looked at his first officer inquisitively. Worf growled. Whatever the answer was, Picard knew he wouldn't like it.

Riker said, "We can't stop because we're cruising at warp eight without using the warp engines."

Chapter Ten

As a Starfleet captain, Picard had experienced many strange things, things that other people might have considered bizarre or even frightening. He was trained to react in a reasoned and appropriate manner to any situation, expected or not. Yet here was a situation that seemed so impossible on the face of it, Picard s first reaction was to be surprised, and then to be disbelieving. While he considered an appropriate response that would be more useful, he marked time by asking a simple question he hoped had a rational answer. "What is our heading, Mr. Crusher?"

"Two two seven mark four, sir."

Riker said, "Back to Tantamon Four."

"Mr. La Forge," Picard called.

"Here, sir."

"What is the condition of our warp engines?"

"Checking, sir." After a moment of silence, La Forge said, "This is impossible, sir."

Picard and Riker shared a glance. Picard said, "What is, Mr. La Forge?"

"We're traveling at warp eight, but the warp engines haven't been engaged."

"Do you have any instant theories, Mr. La Forge?"

"No, sir. But I think this is a little out of the Boogeymen's league."

"Agreed. So far our velocity is not life threatening. Continue to work on the virus."

"Aye, sir."

Riker said, "The teardrop ship we encountered in the Omega Triangulae region traveled at warp speed without a warp drive. According to Data, that ship wasn't even equipped with one."

"Indeed," said Picard. "There is an obvious connection. Moreover, you may recall that the humanoids aboard the teardrop ship were sleeping. Our people began to faint at approximately the same moment the *Enterprise* slipped into warp drive—perhaps at exactly the same moment."

"Another apparent connection."

Picard nodded. "Yet the *Enterprise* is not an alien ship. It has not the means to move at warp speed without using the warp engines."

"Evidently it does," Riker said. He didn't look happy about it. Picard knew that he took every technical puzzle as a personal challenge, sometimes as a personal affront.

Worf said, "The only teardrop ship in this area that we are aware of is the one on Tantamon Four."

"Which is where the *Enterprise* is taking us," Riker said.

Picard shook his head. "But why now?" he said.

The bridge was silent for a moment. The stars on the main viewer poured toward them.

"What about the virus?" Riker said.

"Yes, what about the virus?" Picard said. He had guesses, theories, many questions, but no answers. Nothing he could act on. A frustrating, frustrating business. He stood up, pulled his tunic straight, and walked toward the turbolift. He said, "The crew members who seem to be in the most immediate danger are the ones who fainted. I'm going to sickbay. Call me immediately if our situation changes."

"Aye, Captain."

Picard got on the turbolift and said, "Sickbay." The doors closed, opened, closed again, and then a Boogeyman laughed menacingly. It said "sickbay" over and over in a range of voices from a rumble to a squeak. While Picard wondered if he should have taken the emergency gangway, the turbolift jerked along. A few times Picard's weight seemed to change, and for a few seconds he floated near the ceiling. At last the turbolift doors opened and he stepped out, noting that the lift had stopped a few centimeters above the floor of the corridor.

Picard walked along the corridor. Some of the illumination bars were brighter than usual. Others were dimmer. Some could not seem to make up their mind what to do. Picard was about to enter sickbay when the lights went out entirely, leaving him in a darkness more total than any he had ever seen. Picard imagined the blackness pressing against his eyes.

While afterimages popped like fireworks, he heard somebody shout, "Emergency on deck twelve." Blue emergency lights came on, making the corridor look diseased and unreal, and then the normal lighting blinked on.

A yeoman whose name he didn't know said, "What's going on, sir?"

"The Boogeymen are flexing their muscles," Picard muttered and ducked into sickbay before he would feel obligated to explain.

Sickbay was crowded. Every diagnostic bed was taken, and many crew members and passengers were lying on the floor. They all seemed to be peacefully sleeping. Solemn doctors and orderlies rushed around with medical tricorders and sensing devices. Some were ministering to the sleeping with arcane medical instruments Picard only vaguely recognized. There was a lot of noise, but the patients didn't seem to be in any danger of awakening.

Ravel's *Bolero* began to play. It came in with a crash and then faded to almost nothing. It played too fast and then too slow. Lights flashed in time with the beat. Evidently the Boogeymen were not great respecters of music.

Picard had come down to see if Troi and Baldwin were all right, or at least stable, but it was obvious he could not allow himself the luxury of having personal concerns at this time. Troi and Baldwin were just two among many. He found Dr. Crusher waving a medical sensor over a crewman first class who normally worked in Ten Forward.

When she saw Picard, Dr. Crusher lowered her sensor, though she still looked worriedly at the crewman first class. She took a deep breath and said,

"Before you ask, it's happening to people all over the ship. They're falling into a trance, and I don't know why."

"Any common factor?"

"I don't know yet." Dr. Crusher sounded frustrated, more with herself than with Picard. "So far I'm just trying to make sure no one is dying."

"What is their condition?"

"As far as I can tell, they're just sleeping. But it's a heavy sleep. They can't be awakened, not even by that terrible music, evidently. Can't you control your ship?"

"I'll make it my highest priority," Picard said and gave her a bemused smile.

"Sorry, Captain." Dr. Crusher shook her head with despair. "I'll have some answers for you soon." She began to make passes with her sensor over the crewman again.

Picard wanted to ask her if there was a connection between the trance state and the warp speed, but she obviously had enough on her hands at the moment. Instead, he said, "How are Professor Baldwin and Counselor Troi?"

"Sleeping like the rest of them."

Picard nodded, though it was little more than an automatic social gesture. "Soon," he ordered.

Dr. Crusher nodded absentmindedly. By this time she was diagnosing someone else.

Knowing he was gambling, Picard took the turbolift back to deck one. He won his bet. The ride was astonishingly uneventful.

All seemed quiet on the bridge when he got there, though Riker was pacing and casting angry glances at

154

the main viewscreen, as if it were the source of their trouble. Worf was glaring at the telltales on the tactical rail, probably keeping track of his security systems. He was not a happy Klingon, having been confronted with enemies he felt powerless against. His big dark hands gripped the rail hard.

Bridge functions were the most heavily shielded on the ship. Apparently the Boogeymen were having trouble getting control of them. But if they were in the main core, they could eventually gain control of everything.

Picard sat down in his command chair and rubbed his chin while he watched the screen. None of this made sense. It seemed to him that no program, no matter how renegade, could push a starship at warp speed without using the warp drive. Therefore the Boogeymen could not be responsible. What about the virus? Picard shook his head. Then what was the cause? The trance state of his people? Even if that was the case, he was still left with a very large question. Perhaps Dr. Crusher would discover something.

If Baldwin had been there he could probably have cleared up some of this, but he wasn't, and wishing would not make it so. It was easy to think of him as a casualty of his own deeds, but Picard saw no way that the virus could have anything to do with either the capricious speed of the ship or the spell of sleep that had fallen over selected passengers and crew. Then Picard realized he was not using all his resources.

He raised his voice and said, "Lieutenant Shubunkin."

"Here, Captain."

"Please come to the bridge immediately."

"Now, Captain? Without Baldwin to help me analyze this data, my time is extremely valuable."

"Now, Shubunkin," Riker said.

Sounding slightly miffed, Shubunkin said, "Aye, Commander. Now."

Riker sat down and pulled his tunic straight. He and Picard said nothing. Wesley turned around and said, "Sir, do you think the natives of Tantamon Four have something to do with the warp speed?"

Picard said, "That's what we're hoping Lieutenant Shubunkin will tell us."

Shubunkin arrived on the bridge, huffing and puffing with his own importance. When he saw the stony looks on the faces of Picard and Riker, he calmed down and said, "How can I help you, Captain?"

"Sit down, Lieutenant," Picard said, and indicated the seat normally filled by Counselor Troi.

Shubunkin sat.

Riker said, "Lieutenant, the *Enterprise* is no longer on course for Memory Alpha."

"But—" Shubunkin began. He stopped when Riker held up one hand.

Riker said, "We are cruising back to Tantamon Four at warp eight. The thing that makes this odd is that our warp engines are no longer engaged."

"Isn't that impossible?"

"Yes, it is."

Picard saw that Riker was enjoying baiting Shubunkin, just as he'd enjoyed arguing with him at that first dinner. Riker did not suffer pomposity gladly. However, in this instance, perhaps more could be accomplished by being direct. Picard said, "We don't know how it's being done. Is it possible the natives on Tantamon Four are responsible?"

"Why them?"

"We're going to Tantamon Four," Picard said. "Maybe they want something on the *Enterprise*. Perhaps they want the ship itself."

The idea obviously came as a shock to Shubunkin. He frowned. He looked at the viewscreen. Anything not to be looking at Picard and Riker. Then he met their eyes and said, "I'd just be guessing. Why not ask Baldwin?"

"We're asking you," Riker said.

Shubunkin drew himself up and became very professional. He said, "I'd have to say no. Despite the argument that you saw, Captain Picard, Baldwin and I agree on many things. One of them is the primitive nature of the Tantamon Four natives."

Picard said, "The Orma seem to be primitive, but they have enormous telekinetic powers. They carry their technology in their brains."

Shubunkin shook his head and said, "I don't think that's the case on Tantamon Four. I don't think Baldwin thinks so. By the way, where is Baldwin?"

"Sleeping," said Picard. He explained what had happened as far as he understood it.

"No," said Shubunkin. "That is not the doing of the Tantamon Four natives."

Picard had expected that, and Shubunkin's comment gave him a certain satisfaction. Nothing else seemed to make sense. He said, "What about the teardrop ship?"

"What about it?"

"Could something on that ship be controlling the *Enterprise* or the people aboard?"

"In what way?"

"We were hoping you could tell us," Riker said.

Shubunkin stood up and said, "Despite what you may think of me, sir, I'm good at my job. But I am not a magician. I've had access to Baldwin's infowafer for less than a week. There are many things about the teardrop ship I have not yet discovered."

"Please, Lieutenant," Picard said, "I assure you we all have the highest regard for your abilities."

"Thank you, Captain. Will there be anything else?"

Riker said, "In Professor Baldwin's infowafer, is there any mention of a computer virus?"

Still a bit stiffly, Shubunkin said, "Not that I'm aware of. Of course, I've only scratched the surface. Why?"

Picard said, "Thank you, Lieutenant Shubunkin. You had better return to your work. We'll be getting to Memory Alpha sooner or later. You want to be ready with your report."

"But—"

"Thank you, Lieutenant. Number One, Mr. Crusher, come with me. Mr. Worf, you have the bridge." Picard moved quickly to his ready room, Riker and Wesley following, leaving Shubunkin glaring after them. Picard heard Worf suggest that Shubunkin move along.

Picard touched a companel near his desk. "Dr. Crusher?"

"Here, Captain."

"Anything to report?"

"A few things of interest," Dr. Crusher said carefully. "It's like a dormitory down here."

"Please come to my ready room."

"On my way, sir."

Picard sat down behind the desk and said, "Mr. Crusher, both Data and Mr. La Forge are hard at work on the virus program, so you are here representing the science department."

"Yes, sir," Wesley said with all the seriousness of a young man who knew seriousness was called for.

"Somebody's at the door," a Boogeyman said, and everybody jumped.

"I don't think I'll ever get used to that," Picard said. "Come."

Dr. Crusher walked in looking harried and tired. As she entered, she realized she was carrying a tricorder and slipped it into one of the big pockets of her smock.

"Sit down, Dr. Crusher. I hope that you have something interesting to tell us."

"Interesting, yes. Helpful, I'm not so sure." She sank onto the couch across the room from Picard's desk and said, "I've cross-referenced the records of all personnel in a trance." She smiled wanly. "It took a long time using only tricorders."

"Go on, Doctor," Picard said gently.

"All of them have telepathic indexes that are much higher than normal. Counselor Troi's is the highest, but others are almost as high."

"But why are they in a trance?" Riker said.

"That, Commander, I do not know."

"Could something outside the *Enterprise*, something like the teardrop ship on Tantamon Four, be responsible for it?"

Dr. Crusher looked surprised at the question and then shook her head. After a deep sigh, she said, "But I do know this: alpha and delta waves indicate they are all in deep sleep, the kind you might experience in the middle of the night if you were getting a good rest. Activity in the hypothalamus is normal. However"—she sat forward on the couch, excited by her own revelations—"activity in the Martinez node of the thalamus makes a medical tricorder light up like a Christmas tree."

"What goes on in the Martinez node?" Riker said.

"As far as we knew before, primitive emotional responses."

"And now?"

"I don't know." She massaged her forehead as she went on. "The activity is entirely unexpected. I've never seen anything like it. The Martinez node seems to be coordinating a complex interaction between the cerebellum, which deals with movement, and the thalamus, which is the site of a crude form of consciousness. They are all very busy, but I have no idea what at."

After a short silence, during which Dr. Crusher slumped back on the couch, obviously very tired, Picard said, "Is it possible that the Martinez node is being stimulated by alien influences?"

Wesley said, "If so, it's hard to see why. All those people are doing is sleeping."

"Doctor?" Picard said.

"I'm with Wesley. First contact is always a surprising business. Some unknown individual or race might be doing this, but it *is* difficult to see how they benefit."

As a challenge, Riker said, "We are cruising at warp eight without the warp engines."

Dr. Crusher's eyebrows went up. She looked over at Wesley and he nodded. She said, "You think there's a connection?"

"The Boogeymen and that virus are giving us big trouble, but they are not supernatural."

Wesley allowed himself a smile. "Sir, are you suggesting that the *Enterprise* is haunted?"

"No," said Riker very seriously. "I'm just suggesting that I can't see a connection between our speed and our computer problems."

Dr. Crusher nodded, considering.

"Dr. Crusher," Picard said, "as far as we have been able to determine, people fainted and the *Enterprise* slipped into warp at about the same time. Isn't that correct, Mr. Crusher?"

Wesley nodded. "I heard Commander Riker call out Counselor Troi's name the same second I noticed our new velocity."

Picard said, "Also, the trance of our people is very much like the mental state of the humanoids aboard the teardrop we encountered out in the Omega Triangulae region. What is your opinion, Doctor?"

Dr. Crusher squared her shoulders and sat up a little straighter. She said, "My opinion, Captain, is that from the little I know about warp technology, nothing on this ship can make us go faster than the speed of light except the warp engines themselves. On the other hand, there's still a lot about the human brain we don't know."

"Succinctly put. Number One?"

"What about the influence of the ship back on Tantamon Four?"

Dr. Crusher shrugged. "Unknown."

Riker nodded and said, "Except for the activity in the Martinez node, all the sleepers are sleeping normally?"

"As far as we can tell, yes."

"Then I suggest we sedate them. Knock out the Martinez node."

Dr. Crusher nodded. "As one of my old professors used to say when unusual procedures were suggested, 'It couldn't hurt.'"

"Mr. Crusher?" Picard said.

Wesley had been deep in thought, and he jumped when Picard called his name. "Sorry, sir. I was just wondering where Professor Baldwin got that virus program."

"Maybe he wrote it himself," Riker said.

"Maybe," said Wesley. "If Mom—Dr. Crusher agrees that sedating the sleepers won't hurt them, then it sounds like a good plan to me."

"Agreed," said Picard. "Doctor, make it so."

They went back out onto the bridge, and Wesley took his post at the conn. After a brief hesitation, Dr. Crusher stepped into the turbolift. Picard wondered how long it would be before the turbolifts did not work at all. He said, "Situation normal, Mr. Worf?"

"In a manner of speaking, sir."

The turbolift opened, and La Forge crawled from inside it.

"Trouble, Mr. La Forge?" Riker said.

As he got to his feet, La Forge said, "Yes, sir, but I'm getting used to it. I have an update, sir."

"Good news, I hope."

"News, anyway. Data and I discovered that the machete program didn't clean out the Boogeyman-virus combination because the machete program didn't recognize the virus as a program."

Wesley turned around to look at La Forge who had everybody's attention, even Worf's. Picard said, "An unusual program, is it, Mr. La Forge?"

"You bet, sir." La Forge began to make shapes in the air with his hands. "I've never seen anything like it. The machete program just rolled right over it. Or the combination Boogeyman–exotic virus program managed to hide from the machete program, I'm not sure which. The machete program is not designed to hunt for a moving program, only to erase sitting ducks."

Picard thought about Baldwin, his virus, and his desire to disappear. He said, "Could this exotic virus have come from the teardrop ship Professor Baldwin was studying on Tantamon Four?"

"Absolutely. It could have."

"Find out if there is anything comparable on that infowafer Professor Baldwin brought on board."

"Aye, sir."

Riker said, "Make sure that Shubunkin knows your request for the infowafer comes from the captain."

La Forge smiled. "Aye, sir." When the turbolift doors opened, he looked into the chamber warily, then got on.

The comlink twinkled—fortunately the twinkle had not yet changed into an announcement from a Boogeyman—and Dr. Crusher said, "Captain?"

"Here, Doctor. What have you found?"

"I chose ten subjects at random, Captain, and shot them as full of morphox as I dared. Rapid eye movement stopped immediately, and they went into a deep, dreamless sleep. But the activity in the Martinez node continued."

"No way to shut it off?" Riker said.

"It's a very primitive part of the brain, sir. I see no way to get at it short of murdering the subject."

Picard said, "Thank you, Doctor. We will find another method."

"Aye, sir. Crusher out."

Picard said, "Any change in velocity, Mr. Crusher?"

"No, sir. On course for Tantamon Four at warp eight."

"Damned curious," Picard said.

From behind him came the rumbling voice of Lieutenant Worf. "Sir?"

"What is it, Worf?" Riker said.

"I know why we're going back to Tantamon Four."

Chapter Eleven

PICARD STOOD UP and looked at Worf with an innocent expression. "I assure you," he said, "you have our complete attention."

Worf was impervious to that sort of humor. He merely reported, "Audio transmission coming in from Tantamon Four."

"Let us hear it," Picard said.

The signal sounded like insects playing insect instruments. It had the same charm, the same sound as the signal from the d'Ort'd teardrop ship that had brought them out to the Omega Triangulae region the first time. Picard let it continue while he tried to make sense out of it. He would have left that job to the computer, but he had no great confidence in the computer at the moment.

"Stores," Picard called out.

"Stores. Ward here, sir."

"Mr. Ward, send a tricorder up to the bridge immediately."

"Aye, sir. Ward out."

While the alien music continued, Picard said, "How long has this been going on?"

"Unknown, sir," said Worf. "It is not among the frequencies we normally scan for. I discovered it largely by accident."

Riker's eyebrows went up, and Picard knew why. Worf did not make such an admission lightly.

The turbolift arrived, and the person inside said, "Sir?" as if a little frightened. And with good reason. Ward was standing with his feet flat against the ceiling of the car. Worf and Riker got him down, a tricky job since the Boogeymen had apparently inverted the artificial gravity in that single turbolift.

Picard gave the tricorder to Wesley and ordered him to see if he could make the music yield a message. While Ward went away on the turbolift—oriented normally for the moment—Wesley took a sample of the alien sound. He sat down at the conn, all the while pushing buttons on the tricorder and studying the results.

Mr. Worf's discovery of the alien signal had triggered many thoughts in Picard's head, and for the first time since he and Wesley and Data had emerged from the holodeck, the thoughts led him to conclusions that made sense. While half listening to Wesley tinker with the insect music, Picard matched the evidence together in his head and was delighted to discover that the fit was firm. He looked up and saw Riker watching him.

Earnestly, Picard said, "Number One, I feel that things are coming to a head. The virus seems to have originated aboard the d'Ort'd teardrop ship, although Professor Baldwin may have modified the program for his own use. We are receiving a signal from Tantamon Four that could be coming only from the d'Ort'd ship. We are traveling at warp speed without using our engines, which is something at least one d'Ort'd ship has demonstrated the ability to do. Evidence strongly suggests that the sleepers and the Martinez node have something to do with our speed. Which means that the trance state also has something to do with the d'Ort'd. How does this sound to you, Number One?"

"Good so far, sir."

"Then the d'Ort'd are the key. Perhaps using that key we can reduce our many problems to one."

"Unfortunately," said Riker, "the galaxy's leading expert on the d'Ort'd is in a trance down in sickbay."

"Yes. We will have to make do with Shubunkin."

"He really does know his stuff, sir."

"Glad you realize that. Call a meeting of everyone involved. The conference lounge in ten minutes."

Picard sat at the head of the table, Riker at his right hand. La Forge, Data, Dr. Crusher, and Shubunkin were ranged down the table waiting coolly for him to begin. He wished Troi were there, stabilizing them, reminding them of the human part of the equation if they should ever forget. Still, he felt better now that the problems all had handles, the same handle, the d'Ort'd. Together, he and his staff would save the ship. He only hoped they figured out how to do so before the Boogeymen took total control.

Picard said, "As I see it, we have three problems. First, and perhaps most critical, a virus has attacked our computer and is taking over the ship. Even our main core is at risk. The virus seems to be compounded from an alien program and a program written at the request of Ensign Crusher. It was designed to generate warlike aliens on the holodeck and now seems to be doing that job inside our main computer.

"Second, the *Enterprise* is traveling at warp eight back to Tantamon Four and will arrive there soon. Our warp engines are not engaged. At the same time we are receiving a signal from Tantamon Four that could be coming only from the d'Ort'd ship.

"Third, crew members and civilians are in some kind of trance. An unmapped part of their brains, the Martinez node, is showing unusual activity. Were it not for the fact that this unusual activity seems to have a bearing on our uncontrolled warp, I would say that the rest our sleeping shipmates are getting is the least of our problems. Dr. Crusher?"

"It's true, the sleepers don't seem to be in any danger."

"Very well. Mr. La Forge? Mr. Data?"

Data nodded at La Forge, who stood up and began to explain things. He said, "The combined Boogeymen-d'Ort'd program is unlike anything either Data or I have ever seen. Unfortunately, it is also unlike anything our maintenance programs have seen. That's the reason the virus program is still in the computer and able to get comfy."

Data said, "Analysis of the contagion pattern makes it eighty-five percent certain that the d'Ort'd virus program entered *Enterprise* systems through the terminal in the exobiology lab on deck five."

"The d'Ort'd set out to destroy us," Riker said.

Shubunkin said, "I am sorry to disagree with you, Commander. But I have read Professor Baldwin's extracts and summaries of his work on the teardrop, and I find no evidence of hostile or belligerent tendencies among the d'Ort'd."

"Could they have been hiding their hostile or belligerent tendencies?" Riker said with a hint of sarcasm.

"Possible, but unlikely. It is not consistent with the pattern we have observed among races in our galaxy."

Riker did not appear to be convinced, but he let the matter go.

"Then Baldwin must be responsible," Picard said. He had hoped to find clues to the contrary, but evidently it was not to be.

"Indeed, sir," Data said.

La Forge said, "We have no idea whether the contagion was installed intentionally or not."

Riker said, "At the moment I don't think that's our most urgent question."

"Indeed not," said Data. "But to continue. Mr. La Forge has spent some time telling me about Professor Baldwin, whom I forgot after plugging into the main computer manifested on the holodeck. Mr. La Forge and I have determined that my forgetting was no fluke. The alien virus was modified to wipe any mention of Professor Baldwin from Federation computer records."

Picard said, "Can you flush the Boogeymen-d'Ort'd program from our computer?"

La Forge looked embarrassed. He sat down and said, "Not at the moment, sir."

"I trust you will continue your best efforts."

"Yes, sir."

"Commander Riker, inform Starfleet of our problem and suggest any ships that may come in contact with a d'Ort'd teardrop proceed with great caution."

Data said, "I am afraid, sir, that that is not advisable."

"Why not?" said Riker.

"Anything we broadcast will contain the Boogeymen-d'Ort'd virus. With our first communication, we would doom the Federation."

After a moment of horrified silence, Picard said, "Thank you, Mr. Data. Belay that order, Number One. Let us continue."

Shubunkin said, "If I may?"

"Please," Picard said.

Shubunkin nodded and said, "The sensor readings we took on our first meeting with the teardrop indicated that the d'Ort'd were really two separate races. One was almost human, and the other was so unusual as to be incomprehensible. I would like to propose a theory now that, though strange, fits all the facts as we know them. Please consider it before you reject it."

"Go ahead," said Riker.

"I would like to suggest that the humanoids we observed with our sensors are not the crew of the ship but part of the ship itself."

"How do you mean?" said Dr. Crusher.

"I would like to suggest that the humanoids are used as pushers, to push the teardrop ship into warp." Shubunkin was embarrassed. "Professor Baldwin was correct when he insisted that the d'Ort'd think of the humanoids the same way they think of their tools. Well, that's the reason why."

No one liked the idea very much. It made Picard uncomfortable to think of people being used as tools, no more important than wrenches or dilithium crystals. It was even worse than thinking of Data as just a machine. But the captain could concoct no argument against Shubunkin's theory. No one else spoke up, either. Picard said, "Is it possible, Doctor? Could stimulating the Martinez nodes push a ship into warp?"

"I wouldn't have thought so, but given the evidence —the timing of the fainting and the boost into warp, the high activity of the Martinez nodes—it seems likely. On the other hand, we're on dangerous ground here. Could you look at a human foot and predict ballroom dancing?"

There were guffaws all around the table, in which Shubunkin did not join.

Riker said, "If Lieutenant Shubunkin's theory is correct, it would explain the signal from Tantamon Four. Maybe its purpose is to stimulate people with high telepathic indexes into becoming pushers and to guide them back to the planet."

La Forge said, "What I want to know is how a signal coming all the way from Tantamon Four can cause an effect of that magnitude."

Everyone looked at Dr. Crusher, and she shifted in her chair. "I have a theory almost as strange as Shubunkin's."

"This seems to be the day for it," La Forge said.

Dr. Crusher plunged ahead. "We know from sensor scans that the creatures the d'Ort'd use to push their ships are within two points of being human. Maybe we and they come from the same stock. Maybe the

Martinez node has been a hair trigger waiting millennia for something that would set it off, something like the signal coming from the teardrop on Tantamon Four. The effect of the signal is actually very small, like the pebble that starts the avalanche."

"You mean," said Riker, "the signal set off a reflex?"

Not very happily, Dr. Crusher nodded.

After a moment of silence, Picard swallowed and said, "What you suggest will cause historical and philosophical earthquakes all through the Federation."

Dr. Crusher shrugged and said, "It fits the facts as we know them. I, for one, would be delighted to hear a less bizarre theory."

"We will work on a new theory when we have the time," Picard said. He turned to Shubunkin. "There are no humanoids aboard the teardrop on Tantamon Four?"

"That is right," said Shubunkin. "None of the other creatures, either, if Professor Baldwin is correct."

"Then who is sending the signal?" Data said.

"It could be automated," said La Forge.

Riker shook his head. "But why send the signal now?"

"Because," said Picard, "now the ship has found new pushers."

It took a moment for Picard's statement to sink in, and then Dr. Crusher said, "You mean the teardrop plans to re-man itself with members of the *Enterprise*'s crew? Members selected because of their aptitude to be pushers?"

Everyone looked at Shubunkin. He waited, milking

the moment for its drama. And then he said, "I believe Dr. Crusher has, as you say, hit the screw on the head."

"But how did the d'Ort'd know when to start signaling?" Riker asked.

Dr. Crusher said, "Maybe Baldwin acted as an antenna for their sensors—they must have them even if the sensors are not like ours. The d'Ort'd knew the *Enterprise* was loaded with potential pushers."

"Another bizarre theory," Shubunkin said.

"I'll be damned," said Picard. He slapped the arms of his chair and stood up. "Very well," he said. "Mr. La Forge and Mr. Data, continue your analysis of the Boogeymen-d'Ort'd virus. Draft Ensign Crusher if you believe he would be of use to you. I do not think I need to remind you that time is very much of the essence."

"Yes, sir," La Forge said. He and Data hurried out.

"Dr. Crusher, find a way to deactivate the Martinez node without killing the subject."

"Aye, Captain." Dr. Crusher was on her way to the door when Picard heard the comlink twinkle. Everyone stopped and waited.

"Bridge to Captain Picard," Wesley said.

"Here, Mr. Crusher."

"*Enterprise* has dropped out of warp a hundred thousand klicks off Tantamon Four."

The twinkle came again. "Sickbay to Dr. Crusher." It was a male voice Picard did not know.

Dr. Crusher looked at Picard wonderingly and said, "Go ahead, Birnberg."

"Doctor, the sleepers are awakening."

"And demanding breakfast, no doubt," Riker said.

"Why, yes, sir."

"Feed them," said Dr. Crusher. "Give them anything they want that the food slots are willing to produce. But don't let them fall back asleep. I'll be there in a minute."

"Captain?" Wesley said.

"Patience, Mr. Crusher. Doctor, it is still important for you to find a way to neutralize the Martinez node. We don't want to be at the mercy of the d'Ort'd."

"Aye, sir."

Even before she was gone, Picard said, "Mr. Crusher?"

"Here, sir."

"Make standard orbit around Tantamon Four. The answers to all our questions may be here."

Riker said, "Mr. Worf."

"Here, sir."

"Put guards at all transporters and shuttle bays. We don't want anyone leaving the ship on a d'Ort'd whim."

"Aye, sir. Bridge out."

"What should I do?" Shubunkin said.

"Come with me," Picard said. "We're going to sickbay."

Chapter Twelve

GETTING TO SICKBAY was an adventure. First the turbolift went very fast. Then it went very slowly. Then it rattled along, shaking from side to side like a car in an old-fashioned steam-powered train.

The turbolift stopped first at deck eleven, and a Boogeyman said, "All ashore that's going ashore! We won!"

"Deck twelve," Picard said in what he hoped was a convincing way. The doors closed, and the lift dropped a floor as if the cables had been cut. The turbolift had no cables, but that was what it felt like. The doors opened and then shut quickly, almost pinching Picard in half as he exited into the corridor.

Sickbay was nearly empty by the time he and Shubunkin got there. Dr. Crusher, Counselor Troi, and a few orderlies were moving among those still in bed, mostly children, giving comfort where they could. When Picard approached Troi, she was hugging a small blond girl, rocking with her, telling her that everything would be all right. Troi saw the captain and Shubunkin and said to the little girl, "There. You'll be fine now. Why don't you lie down until you feel ready to go home?"

The little girl sniffed and nodded and did as she was told.

Picard and Shubunkin spoke with Troi near an empty bed where they would be out of the way. "What's wrong with them?" Picard said, a little more gruffly than he had planned.

"Nothing, physically, as far as Dr. Crusher can determine. But if this little girl's dreams were anything like mine, she has a right to be frightened."

"Tell me about the dreams," Shubunkin said.

Troi looked off and frowned. She shook her head and said, "Very alien. Mostly swirling colors. The perspective seemed all wrong, somehow."

"Wrong?" Shubunkin said.

"It would be like explaining sight to a blind person." Troi almost smiled and then shook her head. "Part of the dream was a powerful longing for home."

"Home?" said Picard. "Betazed?"

"Nothing so specific, Captain. But we all felt a definite desire to return to a place that is far away in time and space."

Picard said, "Perhaps that's why you and the others were pushing *Enterprise* at warp eight."

"I thought that was just a rumor," Troi said unhappily.

"It is all too real, I assure you. We need to know

how it was done, not only because in itself it is a tremendous scientific discovery, but because we want to prevent the d'Ort'd from doing it to us again."

Troi thought for a few moments, then shook her head. "I'm sorry, Captain. It's all very vague."

"Try," Picard said.

"Try," Shubunkin said.

Troi sighed and said, "We changed the way we looked at the universe and imposed that new perspective on the ship."

"Explain this new perspective," Picard and Shubunkin said together.

"I'm sorry," Troi said, looking as if she meant it. "I cannot." Her hands moved restlessly. "Details fade like a dream even while I try to remember."

"Perhaps some of the others—" Picard said.

Dr. Crusher interrupted. "I've been asking every one of them I can catch." Picard and Shubunkin turned to look at her. She said, "They don't remember any more than Counselor Troi does, and many of them remember even less. Fortunately, the longing for home fades as quickly as the new perspective. Fortunately also"—she aimed her medical tricorder at Troi and when it warbled, she checked the reading—"the activity in everyone's Martinez node is normal again, which is to say almost nonexistent."

Picard said, "Can you keep it that way?"

"Not yet," Dr. Crusher said, "but we're working on it." She looked somewhat doubtful.

"Very well, Doctor. Flank speed if you please. What do you make of all this, Lieutenant Shubunkin?"

"Nothing useful, Captain. But I am as new to

d'Ort'd psychology and technology as you are. I can only hope that Baldwin's infowafer holds some answers."

"I believe you have just defined your mission, Lieutenant."

"Aye, sir," Shubunkin said and left sickbay at a nice clip.

"Speaking of which," Picard said, "where is Professor Baldwin?"

"He said he was going to see you in your ready room."

That surprised him. The last time he'd seen Baldwin, Picard had accused him of sabotaging the *Enterprise*. "Did he say why?"

"No. But he was most insistent."

Picard touched a companel and said, "Professor Baldwin, this is Picard."

The sound of Boogeymen singing the Hallelujah Chorus poured briefly from the companel. With disgust, Picard said, "Do all you can, Doctor," and strode from sickbay.

As he walked along the corridor to the turbolift, the light bars began to blink. Boogeyman laughter rolled along the corridor like bowling balls, and the ship shuddered. Picard ran to a companel. On his way he moved through a very cold area no larger than a transporter plate. He stepped back into it briefly and saw his breath fog, curl, and dissipate. This was maddening.

He touched the companel and called, "La Forge? What's going on down there?"

"Right offhand, sir, I'd say we have a bad case of Boogeymen."

"Sir, this is Wesley. I think it's going to get worse. I had Data design the Boogeymen to become more aggressive with time."

"Is there no way to go around them?"

"That becomes more and more difficult as the contamination spreads," La Forge said. "We don't have many options left."

"Make use of those we do have. Picard out."

There was no point being angry at La Forge. He and Data and Wesley were doing the best they could, which, Picard knew, was the best that anyone could do. If only it hadn't been for Baldwin and his damned compulsion to disappear. Baldwin was in his ready room. Maybe he had an answer. Picard kept moving.

Suddenly the corridor tilted sharply, rolling Picard head over heels back the way he had come. He banged into the wall at the T-intersection and tried to collect his wits. Ensign Perry was next to him, evidently trying to do the same thing. She was a tall, slim blonde with short hair and good cheekbones. Picard made sure that she was all right, and together they stared along the corridor at the turbolift at the other end, a direction that had suddenly become a steep upward grade.

"What's going on, sir?" Perry said.

The Boogeymen were growing stronger; that was what was going on. But to explain the Boogeymen to Perry would take a while, and Picard did not feel he had the time to spare. He said, "We have a computer problem. Senior staff is working toward a solution at this moment."

"Yes, sir." Perry tried on a smile. It was becoming but not hopeful. She didn't understand but was attempting to take Picard's answer at face value. He took it at face value himself and hoped he was correct.

"Come along, Ensign. Perhaps the floor will level out farther on." Picard helped her crawl up the floor. It was textured to give maximum traction when walking, but no one in Starfleet Engineering had guessed that anyone would ever need to climb it. They rested opposite sickbay, sitting against the corridor wall and catching their breath.

Inside sickbay, Dr. Crusher was walking around normally. When she saw them, she came to the doorway and said, "Boogeymen?"

"Yes," said Picard. "We can no longer make assumptions about the operation of the ship. Stay in sickbay unless you must make an emergency call, and pray that the Boogeymen leave you alone."

"Yes, sir. Can I help you or Ensign Perry in any way?"

Ensign Perry swallowed and attempted a game smile. She said, "I'll be fine."

"We will all be fine," Picard said with more conviction than he felt.

Picard and Perry continued their climb. When they were not far past sickbay the gravity tilted again, and threw them at the turbolift. The doors opened, and the two of them fetched up inside. The doors closed before they could get to their feet, and the car began to move.

"We win," a Boogeyman said. "Shuttle bay two. Shuttle bay three."

"Where are we going, sir?"

"Computer," Picard called, "bridge."

"The bridge is ours. We win!"

Picard smiled confidently into Perry's terrified face, hoping it would give her comfort, but the truth was, he did not feel confident. Without the main core, functions that normally were automatic would take many crew-hours to monitor, calculate, and adjust. Just watching over life support would be a full-time job. Even Data would need many hours to calculate course and speed to the nearest starbase.

Picard thought of a useful analogy that was not encouraging. It was as if a human suddenly had to consciously, second by second, will every electrochemical reaction in his or her body or it would not happen. That person would certainly be dead in seconds. The situation aboard the *Enterprise* was not so dire as all that, but soon it would be and the Boogeymen would win in earnest.

The turbolift stopped, the door opened, and Picard was surprised to see they had actually come to the bridge. He leapt out and pulled Ensign Perry after him before the turbolift changed its mind and bore them away to some remote corner of the ship.

Worf was at his station, and Riker sat in the center seat, though at this point, command consisted of watching the disasters pile up. Ensign Winston-Smyth was at Ops. Conn was unmanned.

Picard sat Ensign Perry in Troi's seat and told her she would be safer staying on the bridge than attempting to go somewhere else. She nodded and glumly watched Tantamon IV on the main viewer.

Riker had already moved to his own seat. Picard sat down and said, "Status."

Riker said, "Minor damage reports are coming in from all over the ship. Evidently ship's environment is now under the Boogeymen's control."

"Ensign Perry and I experienced that firsthand. Anything else?"

As if in answer, the ship shuddered, and Picard saw a photon torpedo fly across the main screen. A few seconds later it exploded, briefly washing out the picture with bright light.

"What in hell?" Picard said.

Worf said, "Our photon torpedoes and phasers are firing at random."

"Target?" Picard said.

"None," said Worf.

"I suppose we must be grateful for that," Picard said. A phaser beam momentarily poked and fizzed into the darkness and then stopped abruptly. No one bothered to mention it. Picard said, "Is Baldwin in my ready room?"

"Yes, sir," said Riker. "He said you wanted to see him." He gave Picard a look that was full of meaning.

"Right enough. Keep me posted." He walked to the ready room doors, and they opened for him. They remained open after he walked through. Well, at least he would not have to suffer that new door announcement.

The ready room was dim, as if it were ship's night. The stars out the window behind his desk looked unnaturally bright, though Picard was fairly certain the Boogeymen had not yet been able to tinker with them. Baldwin stood by the window looking out. Without turning around he said, "I thought I'd be safe on your ship, Jean-Luc. Then Mont attempted to kill me, and now the ship itself seems itchy to try."

Picard said, "Has anyone told you about the ship going into warp without using the engines?"

"They did. I didn't believe it."

"Believe it."

Baldwin turned around. The enforced rest had done him no good. He looked thin and drawn even in the low light, which, Picard knew, generally flattered people. "Why do I get the feeling that you think I'm somehow responsible?"

"Sit down, Eric."

Baldwin lit up that shy smile—one of the features, Picard suspected, that so endeared him to women—and came around the desk to sit down.

Picard settled behind his desk. He was glad to see that the fish in the tank on the other side of the room still appeared to be healthy. Its environment was controlled by the same systems that controlled life support on the rest of the ship. Picard suddenly thought of the canaries that used to be taken down into coal mines; because of their delicate constitutions they were the first to fall prey to poisonous gas. Seeing a bird fall gave the workers a good chance of getting out of the pit alive. Fancifully, Picard decided that as long as the fish was all right, the crew of the *Enterprise* still had the same chance as those miners.

Baldwin said, "Last time I was here, you accused me of installing a virus in your computer."

"The evidence is overwhelming at this point, Eric."

"Is it?" Baldwin was still trying to make light of the situation, but his voice shook.

"And the fact that in doing so you've broken any number of Federation laws is not important right now. What is important is for you to tell my chief engineer all you can about it."

Baldwin was quickly losing his polish. Sounding a little shrill, he said, "What can that virus possibly have to do with—"

Picard interrupted. "Somehow your virus program is working in synergy with a program designed to create aggressive, warlike aliens on the holodeck. The resulting mess is destroying my ship."

"I see," Baldwin said. He began to nod and did not stop. His face took on the pained expression of a man who'd been made to confront an unpleasant reality. His breath came hard and fast, and his hands were all a jumble in his lap. He stood up and began to pace. "So I'm responsible for all your troubles."

"Eric, please—"

"I'm sorry, okay? I didn't mean to endanger anyone." The calm, heroic Baldwin was entirely gone. Every part of him shuddered. He was agitated, nearly frenzied.

Trying not to feel guilty about prodding Baldwin into this fit, Picard watched him closely. Baldwin's excitement was building to hysteria. Hoping for the best, Picard touched his insignia and said, "Counselor Troi to the captain's ready room."

"We have your ship now, Captain Crusher," a Boogeyman voice said.

"I just wanted to disappear." Baldwin clutched his face and cried.

"Eric, I . . ." Picard began, wondering what Troi would do if she were there.

Baldwin bolted from the room through the open door. Picard ran after him and almost caught him as he stepped into the forward turbolift. The door closed, nearly chopping Picard's hands off at the wrists. He called, "Mr. Worf, security alert. Professor Baldwin is to be considered dangerous, most of all to himself."

"Aye, Captain." A few seconds later he said, "No response on any comlink channels."

"We'll have to catch him ourselves. Worf, Number One, Ensign Perry, come with me. Ensign Winston-Smyth, you have the bridge."

Winston-Smyth looked horrified, but said, "Aye, sir," and hurriedly turned to her Ops board.

The doors of the forward turbolift would not open and neither would the aft. Worf offered to pry the doors apart with his bare hands, but Picard was not sure even Worf would be able to perform such a feat. All Picard said was, "What is the good if no turbolift car is there?"

Worf growled but saw the logic of Picard's question.

"The emergency gangway," Riker said and headed for an emergency door between the battle bridge turbolift and the main viewscreen.

Picard said, "Number One."

Riker, obviously in a big hurry, turned to look at Picard.

Gently, Picard said, "Number One, where are you going?"

"To find Baldwin." Riker frowned, then smiled ruefully. He said, "He could be anywhere." He tapped his insignia and said, "Computer, where is Professor Baldwin?"

Nothing came from the comlink. Not even Boogeyman laughter.

Worf ran back to his post at the tactical rail and began to punch buttons. He growled and then said, "This is hopeless." He gripped the rail.

"The computer is down?" Perry said.

"Not down," said Riker, "but definitely falling."

"What about using a tricorder?"

Picard considered that idea along with everyone else. He said, "A tricorder's range is limited, and Baldwin could be anywhere on the ship. We could be hunting for a long, long time."

"Perhaps there is a way," Worf said. "With the tricorder on external setting, we might be able to use it and *Enterprise*'s sensor net together."

"Without our tricorder becoming contaminated?" Riker said.

"I believe so. We would not link the tricorder with the ship's computer system. The sensor net would merely be a kind of antenna for the tricorder. The tricorder would do all the actual data processing."

"Very good, Mr. Worf," Picard said.

Perry still looked doubtful. "Where is the nearest tricorder?" she asked.

"Sickbay," said Riker.

"Right you are, Number One. Lead the way."

With a grim, wolfish smile, Riker worked the mechanical lock and pushed open the door to the gangway. Emergency light bars were like blue threads that followed the stairs down. Picard suggested they take flashlights anyway, against the good possibility that the Boogeymen would sense their presence in the stairwell and deprive them of light.

The gangway was an eerie place. The air was cool and dead. No attempt had been made to beautify the place. Cables and conduits lined the walls. The occasional sensing mechanism beeped and flashed. In all his years as captain of the *Enterprise,* this was only the second time Picard had been on the gangway. The first time, it had been part of his welcoming tour.

The metal stairs rang like gongs with each step they took; their shadows jumped and danced, grew and diminished. It was not difficult for Picard to imagine armies of Boogeymen following them or rising from below to meet them.

When they reached deck twelve, Riker manipulated another lock. As he pushed open the door to the corridor, a portable memo screen floated past. A lieutenant swam after it, looking a little green. Starfleet still demanded that all personnel have a zero-g rating, but the skills required to get the rating were not often needed aboard a starship. And with the skills went the discipline of the stomach. When the lieutenant saw Picard, he grabbed one of the ornamental pillars that lined the corridor and said, "We seem to have a gravity leak, sir."

"Gravity leak?" Riker asked.

"Yes, sir. The gravity gradient is gradually decreasing, as if the gravity were running out."

Picard said, "So I see. Very picturesque. Carry on, Lieutenant . . ."

"Hiller, sir."

"Of course. Carry on, Lieutenant Hiller."

The lieutenant nodded, grimaced, and swam toward sickbay.

Picard stepped out of the stairwell and immediately

lost all his weight. His mass remained the same, of course, but that was of less concern to him than the discomfort rising from his stomach and twirling in his brain. For the moment he was not sorry that the food slots were not functioning properly. "Come on," he said, hoping he sounded more encouraging than he felt.

He followed Lieutenant Hiller into sickbay and slowly sank till his feet touched the floor. It was obvious that there was a gravity leak in sickbay, too, but the gravity coils still worked a little, for which he was grateful. Behind him, Riker, Worf, and Perry landed. Worf said, "A warrior was not meant to be a bird."

A few children still lolled around sickbay, but they looked considerably more chipper than Picard felt. Dr. Crusher was using a hypospray on Lieutenant Hiller. When she saw Picard and the others, she said, "Antinausea medicine. Wait right there. The four of you are next."

Troi approached Picard and said, "What is going on, sir?"

Worf growled and said, "Boogeymen."

"They have the ship?"

"Not yet," said Riker.

Dr. Crusher hit Picard in the arm with the hypo, and he heard it hiss. Seconds later his stomach settled and his brain stopped chasing itself. The others looked relieved, too. Picard told Dr. Crusher why they had come to sickbay, and she gave them a tricorder. "With or without the medical attachment?" she asked.

"What is your opinion?" said Picard.

Dr. Crusher shook her head and said, "The tricorder has no information on ship's crew and passengers. You'll have to give it something to look for."

"There are a lot of human males aboard *Enterprise*," Riker said.

"Yes," said Picard, "but I'll wager that none of them are as agitated as Baldwin was when he left my ready room."

"All right. With the medical attachment, then," said Dr. Crusher as she took back the tricorder and adjusted a few settings. She handed the instrument back to Picard. "You'll be fine as long as he's upset. After he calms down, Baldwin will be just one more human male."

Picard handed the tricorder to Worf, who made adjustments of his own. He cast around the room and at last aimed the tricorder at the ceiling. "He is above us," Worf said.

"Transporters?" Riker said.

Picard nodded and said, "They are well guarded."

"He is moving," Worf said as he followed Baldwin with the tricorder. "Coming this way. From his speed, I would guess he is aboard a turbolift."

"How did he do that?" Perry said.

"Friends," said Worf. "The turbolift has stopped. He is just above us."

"Deck eleven," said Riker. "Holodecks."

Picard said, "Thank you, Doctor. You stay here, Counselor. The doctor's patients have need of you. Number One, Perry. After you, Mr. Worf."

Worf swam ahead of Picard, Riker, and Perry down the corridor to the gangway, and they climbed one flight of stairs. Deck eleven was dim and the air was hot and dry, desertlike. But the gravity was within a few points of normal, and they were all glad of that.

According to the tricorder, Baldwin was in holodeck three and just as upset as ever. They continued to get a strong reading. As they approached the entrance, it opened to show them a jungle much like the one on Tantamon IV.

"It appears," said Picard, "that we are being invited inside."

Worf's jaw worked. Perry looked to Picard for guidance. Riker said, "Worf and I will go."

"You're half right, Number One. You and I will go."

"I must insist, sir—"

"Number One, this is not an away mission. For better or worse, holodeck three is part of the ship, my ship."

Looking unhappy, Riker said, "Aye, sir."

Picard said, "Worf, you and Perry wait out here. And stay sharp. Things that can enter a holodeck can also exit."

"Aye, sir," Worf and Perry said together.

Picard took a deep breath and swallowed. He did not consider himself a brave man, but he generally did what needed to be done. Still, if the thought of once more entering a holodeck under control of Boogeymen did not frighten him, at the very least it made him cautious. He studied the jungle warily.

"Sir?" said Riker.

Picard realized he had been studying the jungle for a long time. He said, "Quite right, Number One," and stepped onto the holodeck. Riker was right behind him. The doors closed behind them and disappeared.

Chapter Thirteen

"THIS ISN'T SO BAD," Picard said as they tramped through the steamy undergrowth and among the fuzzy alien bowls. "At least it doesn't look like the *Enterprise*." He saw Baldwin a little way ahead of them, making good time. Picard pointed, Riker nodded, and they followed him through the rising mist.

Though Baldwin started with a lot of energy, he slowed as time went on and Picard could not figure out why. It was true that because of the temperature, the uneven ground, and the vines and bowls, walking was difficult for a man who was used to civilization. But Picard was not yet fatigued, and Baldwin had more experience with this kind of terrain than he did.

His impatience, and perhaps his feeling of responsibility for Picard's well-being, made Riker walk a few steps ahead. He caught up with Baldwin and spun him around by a shoulder. Riker fell back a step, and

Picard stopped. The man they'd been following wasn't Baldwin but a Boogeyman. He laughed maniacally, pushed Riker in the chest, and ran. He had no trouble skimming through the jungle now. Riker watched him go. Picard came up next to Riker and said, "The holodeck is protecting Baldwin."

"But why?" Riker said. He sounded more angry than frustrated.

Before Picard had a chance to respond, a Boogeyman voice behind them cried, "What ho, varlets!" They turned and found themselves under attack by an armored knight wielding a broadsword.

Both Picard and Riker were astonished, but as Picard picked up a stout limb, he saw that Riker was at a total loss. "I keep telling you, Number One," Picard said as they backed away from the knight. "History is important. That includes historical weapons."

The captain stood his ground. The knight rushed at him and swung his sword. Picard parried, and the sword hacked through the tree limb, spitting wood chips.

"You've done this before, sir," Riker said as Picard watched the knight warily.

"Many times. Perhaps that's why the Boogeymen chose this particular scenario."

The knight came at Picard again. The captain could see that this was not a time for chivalry or even for following the formal rules of battle. He ducked inside the arc of the knight's sword and bashed him across the ribs with the stump of his limb.

The knight grunted and tottered backward, unable

to regain his balance. He crashed into a small lime green bowl and lay there, arms and legs waving in the air like an overturned Jode's dust weevil.

Riker leapt forward and pulled open the knight's visor. He pulled his hand away as the thing inside snapped at him. "Another Boogeyman, sir."

"What a surprise. Leave him, Number One. Let's keep moving."

Riker stood up, and the knight disappeared. "What's the point, sir? The holodeck can divert us like this for as long as it likes."

"Perhaps. But it cannot divert Mr. Worf and Ensign Perry. If we are busy, they can catch Baldwin when he tries to leave the holodeck."

Riker nodded, but still looked unhappy. He did not enjoy a waiting game, not even when it was fairly active, like the one presented by the holodeck. He could be subtle if the situation called for it, but waiting was not his style.

They walked on and did not see another soul for a long time. Strange perfumes came and went on the heavy air. Occasionally Picard and Riker heard the shouts of wild animals or saw birdlike creatures rising against the hot silver sky. They were resting against a boulder at one side of a clearing when a Boogeyman stepped out of the jungle. He wore the classic nineteenth-century North American cowboy outfit, including a pistol at either hip. He stepped forward, spurs jingling, hands poised for a quick draw.

"A holodeck favorite?" Picard asked.

"Yes, sir. You see I have an interest in history after

all—the North American Wild West." Riker smiled when he said it.

The gun-toting Boogeyman stopped and said, "I'm calling you out, Riker."

"No, thank you," Riker said to the gunman. He turned as if to leave, and the Boogeyman shot at his feet, causing Riker to flinch. The explosion of the old-fashioned percussion weapon made a covey of birdlike creatures flap into the air.

The Boogeyman said, "You'll draw or you'll dance."

"Enjoy it, Number One," Picard said.

"I don't have—" He looked down and saw that a pair of six-shooters was holstered at his waist. "Historical weapons," he said. He nodded and smiled grimly as he stepped forward.

The Boogeyman came forward to meet him. They faced each other with half the clearing between them.

The Boogeyman said, "You still got a chance, Riker. Leave Baldwin be."

While watching the Boogeyman, Riker whispered over his shoulder at Picard, "We must still have a good chance to find Baldwin if the Boogeymen are trying this hard to dissuade us from searching." Riker turned to the Boogeyman, and called, "Did you come to draw or to talk?"

The Boogeyman smiled, showing one gold tooth in his rotten mouth. Picard did not see him draw, but suddenly a pistol was in his hand, smoking from a single shot. Riker cried out and fell, gripping his leg. Blood flowed between his fingers.

Picard pulled Riker behind the boulder, hoping that the Boogeyman would not follow. He knelt beside Riker, feeling helpless. He touched his insignia and said, "Dr. Crusher to holodeck three. Emergency."

Nothing came over the comlink but the hiss of rushing air.

Riker's face, which had been screwed up in pain, suddenly smoothed. Astonished, Riker smiled with relief. He took his hands away from his leg, and no wound was there. No blood, no ragged hole. He said, "I wonder if they can't hurt us because they don't want to or because they can't entirely surmount the holodeck safeguards."

"Distraction is the name of the game, Number One. I am confident that they will hurt us badly if they feel the need."

While Picard knelt there thinking about the Boogeymen's talent for creating chaos and destruction, another Boogeyman swung through on a vine and dropped in front of them. He wore bell-bottomed leather breeches over thick buckled boots, and a leather vest. A saber hung at his side and a knife was clutched between his rotten teeth. His hair was long, curly, and black, and he wore a gold ring through one of his horns.

They stood up. Riker stepped a little in front of Picard.

The Boogeyman took the knife from his teeth and flipped it as he talked, always catching it by the bone handle. In his harsh voice he said, "Avast there, mates."

"I am Captain Jean-Luc Picard of the Federation starship *Enterprise*."

"Aye," said the pirate. "I know who you be."

"Space pirates?" Riker said wonderingly.

"Aye," said the Boogeyman. Suddenly he menaced

them with the knife. "I be Captain Pilgrim from the Orion Nebula. And you be my prisoners."

Picard remembered such romantic creatures from when he was much younger and had an interest in popular culture. His favorite holoshow had been called "Rim Runners." This Boogeyman would have fit right in.

"A scenario based on a preoccupation of my childhood, Number One. I haven't run it in years."

"A holodeck never forgets," Riker said grimly. He grabbed the wrist of the hand that wielded the knife and tried a little karate, but Captain Pilgrim didn't even waver. He stood there, steady as a statue, and smiled a terrible smile. He said, "Things be different here on the holodeck."

"Perhaps we'd better go with him," Picard said.

"Baldwin is getting away."

"Not very far, I think," said Picard.

"Arrhh," said Captain Pilgrim. "We win. We always win."

He prodded them through the jungle until they came to a spaceship. Though not exactly like the ones on "Rim Runners," this ship had much the same flamboyance and unlikely style. It was as big as a small house and splashed with bright primary colors. The warp engines were festooned with useless but jaunty filigree. Painted on the fin that rose off the back of the elliptical ship was a skull and crossbones.

A door dropped outward on a hinge, and Captain Pilgrim encouraged Picard and Riker up the stairway made by the inside of the door. Inside, the ship was a mad mixture of styles. Brass eighteenth-century orreries, sextants, and telescopes abutted twentieth-century binnacles and Starfleet-issue tricorders. The walls were paneled with wood, and the furniture consisted of couches and overstuffed easy chairs; the couches before the control board might have come off the *Enterprise* herself. Strung from wall to wall were sails and colored flags.

Captain Pilgrim said, "Here you be and here you stay till Professor Baldwin makes his escape."

"We want to help Professor Baldwin," Riker said.

Captain Pilgrim gave a gruff laugh and forced them down a narrow stairway to a small room lit by a single lantern. When Pilgrim lowered the hatch, the room became moist and nearly airless. They could hear Pilgrim clumping around on the deck above.

Picard got comfortable on one of the big sacks stacked against the bulkhead, and said, "You might as well sit down, Number One. I would say we've been captured good and proper."

"Excuse me, sir," said Riker, "but you seem peculiarly relaxed about this situation."

With sudden intensity, Picard said, "Number One, we've already guessed that the d'Ort'd want new pushers for their ship. It's my guess that Baldwin's their first choice. But in order for him to be their pusher, he's going to have to get down to Tantamon Four. And in order to do that—"

"The d'Ort'd are eventually going to have to come to you."

Riker smiled and nodded. He sat down next to Picard, folded his hands, and together they waited.

* * *

Worf stood at ease in front of the holodeck doors while Ensign Perry sat against the wall opposite him. Perry ran a finger around inside her collar and said, "Don't you ever sweat?"

"Yes," said Worf.

After a long silence Ensign Perry said, "You're not sweating now."

Worf made a sigh that sounded like a growl and said, "I am comfortable at the moment, thank you. Generally I am much too cold."

"Doesn't that bother you?"

"I am a warrior."

Perry nodded and said, "I wish I had some water."

Worf just stiffened and ground his teeth.

Perry smiled and said, "Don't you wish you had some water?"

"No."

Perry did her best to look hurt.

A moment later three things happened at once: the holodeck doors slid open, Baldwin leapt through the opening, and Worf turned and caught him. Baldwin struggled hard, but like a child.

"I do not want to have to sit on you," Worf said.

Baldwin's fighting subsided, but Worf still held him. Worf looked around and said, "What's that smell?"

"Skunk," said Perry with surprise.

"Skunk?" said Worf.

"A small Earth animal that smells bad to protect itself. Lot of them near Grangeville, where I grew up. But what's that smell doing on the *Enterprise?*"

"Boogeymen," Worf said.

"What?"

"Come along. We will take Professor Baldwin to the brig for safekeeping."

"No," cried Baldwin. "You must not."

Picard sat on the steps below the hatch listening and waiting. Riker was watching him from across the room. They hadn't heard noise from above for a long time. Without warning the pirate ship disappeared, leaving Picard and Riker standing on a blank holodeck. Blank but for Captain Pilgrim. At the other side of the big room the doors were open, and through them Picard could see Worf clutching Baldwin, who was struggling. Ensign Perry stood nearby, wanting to help but not knowing how.

Captain Pilgrim walked toward them; it was almost a stroll, not the swagger that he'd used before. He spoke in the Boogeyman voice, but it had changed. It was no longer arrogant and evil, but softer, more reasonable. Pilgrim said, "Captain Picard, you must allow Baldwin to beam down to Tantamon Four."

"Whom do I have the honor of addressing?" Picard said.

"We have no individual names. You may call us Pilgrim."

Riker, always quick to get to the point, folded his arms and said, "Who are you, exactly?"

"We are the d'Ort'd."

Picard did not know what the others were doing at that moment. He was too busy dealing with his own astonishment. The d'Ort'd were obviously as alien as the sensors had shown them to be, and someday soon that alienness would be a pretty problem for a specialist like Shubunkin. Anger grew in Picard, and it overwhelmed his astonishment. He said, "Release control of my ship and we can discuss Baldwin."

"Another controls your ship. Not us. We have tried to restrain them."

"The Boogeymen?" Riker asked.

"So you call them."

"Why didn't you communicate with us before?"

"No one came on the holodeck before. Baldwin was not detained before."

Riker gave a short, humorless laugh.

"I was on the holodeck before. With two other crew members."

"For a long time we were in shock. Being installed in an alien computer is stimulating but difficult."

"Not so easy from this side of the terminal either," Riker said. He smiled, but he wasn't joking.

"Can we have a few chairs?" Picard said.

The air wavered and four armchairs off the pirate ship appeared. They faced each other across a small campfire. Picard could smell smoke, hear the wood crackling. Was the fire a trick, a calculated ploy to relax them, or just a nice touch? These chairs, this fire, in the middle of the blank holodeck gave Picard the impression of camping in the middle of a technological wilderness. Perhaps, with the Boogeymen in command, that's all *Enterprise* itself was at the moment. He and Riker sat down. Pilgrim sat across from Picard.

Riker said, "Where are the real d'Ort'd, the creatures who wrote your program?"

"Creatures? Like Baldwin?"

This was taking a very strange turn, Picard thought. He said, "Yes, like Baldwin."

"There are no creatures. We are the d'Ort'd."

Eagerly Picard said, "Number One, if what they say is true, it would explain why we could not find the location of the other set of aliens our sensors detected aboard the original Omega Triangulae teardrop. They have no bodies. They are a computer program."

"Computer programs don't spontaneously generate. Somebody has to write them."

Pilgrim said, "No one wrote us. Our planet has a highly organized crystalline structure. The heat from the molten core is converted to electrical energy. Over millennia, the energy became organized, too. No one wrote us. We evolved."

Contemplatively, almost as if speaking to himself, Picard said, "You were part of the information Baldwin took from the teardrop ship on Tantamon Four. You were on the infowafer he brought aboard."

"We were happy to help Baldwin delete himself from Federation records."

"Why?" Riker said.

Pilgrim said, "We want Baldwin. We need him." A little of the old Boogeyman barbed inflection returned to his voice momentarily.

"To be your pusher?" Picard said.

"Yes. Our organic units died on Tantamon Four. We need Baldwin to be our pusher so that we can go home."

"Only Baldwin?" Riker said.

"Yes. *Enterprise* has no focusing mechanism. Many minds were needed to push your ship back to

Tantamon Four. Our ship has the focusing mechanism. We need only Baldwin to push the ship into warp."

Picard nodded and said, "Knowing that should please Baldwin and Shubunkin." As he had guessed, the d'Ort'd were indeed the key to *Enterprise*'s problems, or at the center of them, anyway. If they were telling the truth about not being able to control the Boogeymen, knowing the d'Ort'd were a living race only made things more complicated.

Riker said, "Baldwin was aboard your ship for months, poking around, doing tests. If you needed him, why did you allow him to leave?"

"We didn't know he was there. We were asleep, awaiting rescue."

"A rescue mission is on its way?"

"Perhaps."

"Enough of this," Picard said. "Before we can discuss Baldwin, I must have control of the *Enterprise*."

"The Boogeymen are in control. We can restrain them, but we cannot stop them. When we decided to help Baldwin erase himself from your records, we let him modify our basic structure for his purposes. That modification allowed your Boogeymen to attach themselves to us."

"So you can't get rid of them either," Riker said.

"That is correct," the d'Ort'd replied. "Nor can we stop spreading through your computer. It is our nature to grow. The Boogeymen grow with us."

Picard wondered again if the d'Ort'd were telling the truth about their powerlessness against the Boogeymen. He decided there was no way to know and therefore it was not worth worrying about till circumstances forced him to do so. He had enough to worry about as it was—and clearly, their first concern was stopping the Boogeymen.

Picard called out, "Mr. Worf, please have Professor Baldwin join us."

Baldwin fought Worf briefly and then went limp. Ensign Perry followed and stood between Picard and Riker. "Sir?" she said.

"Not now, Ensign," Riker said.

Perry looked at Riker, obviously puzzled by his abruptness.

Worf deposited Baldwin like a sack in the extra chair. The exologist seemed gray and shrunken. His hair was not combed or even rakishly disheveled, only in disarray. He was not dirty, but then, *Enterprise* offered few opportunities to get that way. He would not look at them.

"Eric," Picard said as gently as he could. He had to say it again before Baldwin looked up. The eyes, the slackness of his face, everything about him suggested madness.

Picard said, "Eric, we need to know how you changed the d'Ort'd code so that it would erase any mention of you from Federation documents. We need to know so we can save the ship and you and the d'Ort'd."

Baldwin laughed. The laugh was terrible and had no intelligence behind it; it went on and on.

Chapter Fourteen

THE LAUGHTER CONTINUED. It made Picard itch in places he could not reach, inside his brain, up and down his spinal column. From their actions he could tell that the others felt the same way. Even Worf looked anxious. Only Pilgrim, the d'Ort'd persona, sat calmly.

Picard knew that Baldwin, in his present state, was far beyond his reach. None of the other sleepers had suffered what Baldwin was going through. Perhaps it had something to do with being chosen by the d'Ort'd. Or something to do with Baldwin himself. Eventually they would know. It was possible that Starfleet would someday have its own pushers, giving the Federation interstellar travel without warp engines. An age-old dream. The exploration of space would truly become a human adventure at last.

Picard walked to a corner of the big room. The walls absorbed sound and made the laughter seem much farther away than it was. In the relative quiet, Picard heard the *Enterprise* creaking like a ship at sea. Holodeck illusion or more Boogeyman mischief? Could the sound be real, caused by the stress put on the ship by the Boogeymen? Maybe things were even more desperate than he had thought. Ever hopeful, Picard touched his insignia and said, "Sickbay."

"Nobody here by that name," said a Boogeyman.

Picard came back to the overstuffed chairs and ordered Worf to go down to sickbay and bring back Dr. Crusher and Counselor Troi. "Ask Dr. Crusher to bring a complete medikit."

"Aye, Captain."

"What about me, Captain?" Ensign Perry said.

Picard glanced at Worf, but he was stone-faced, as usual. "Very well," said Picard. "Stay sharp."

Worf and Perry left the holodeck together. Did Perry think they were friends? It was possible; human women had been attracted to Worf before. The coolness, the blatant animal magnetism, the sense of humor that he tried mightily to hide—all had admirers. Interesting, but not Picard's business. Maybe she just wanted to get away from Baldwin.

Wesley could not remember being more brain-weary. Yes, he could. He'd once stayed up all night to review his plasma physics notes before the final exam. He'd forced himself to take two hours off for sleep, and it had been enough, but just barely.

He and Geordi and Data were sitting at Engineering's master situation monitor, but not using any of the terminals. If they wanted information or lightning-fast computation, they had to use tricorders.

Testing theories and figuring mathematical answers had become a frustratingly slow process.

"What about this?" La Forge said. "We can create a feedback loop so that whatever the Boogeymen do to the *Enterprise* will come back to bite them."

Data shook his head. "I believe we tried a tricorder simulation of that solution four hours and thirty-seven minutes ago."

"Did it work?" La Forge asked.

Wesley laughed at that, but Data merely said no, which only made Wesley laugh harder. The comical look of confusion on Data's face made La Forge laugh, too. Then he took a deep breath and said, "We're all a little slaphappy, I guess."

All of them except Data. Being an android, he was still alert and fresh. Long after Wesley and La Forge sat staring into space, trying not to lose the trail of some possible but obscure solution, Data was still eagerly punching information into his tricorder.

The three of them sat without talking. The normal sounds of Engineering twittered and bonked around them. Computer screens were blank or were rolling up line after line of gibberish or showing distorted images of Boogeymen. Occasionally a Boogeyman would laugh or make a threat or tell the world that they had won.

At least one good thing had come out of this situation. The Boogeymen, while still disturbing, had ceased to frighten Wesley. Familiarity had diluted their power. He guessed that even if he saw them in his sleep, he would no longer consider the experience a nightmare, but only a mildly unpleasant dream.

La Forge's staff tried to look busy, but they had little to do while the Boogeyman-d'Ort'd virus was in control of the ship. They occupied themselves mainly in staying away from La Forge, Data, and Wesley.

"Gentlemen," Data said.

Both La Forge and Wesley jumped.

La Forge stretched. Wesley opened his eyes very wide while trying to will himself back to alertness. "You have something?"

"I believe I do," said Data. "If we simplify the interface codes between input and lobe one of the mainframe, I believe it will allow a new machete program to access, recognize, and delete the Boogeyman-d'Ort'd virus."

"That's great," said Wesley. The excitement that came with the possibility of success made him feel more awake.

"Let me see that," said La Forge. Data handed him the tricorder. He studied the screen for a while, punched a few buttons, and studied it again. He said, "This'll erase the combination, not just the Boogeymen."

"Correct," Data said.

La Forge puckered his lips and shook his head. "I don't know, Data. If what Captain Picard guessed is true, the d'Ort'd virus is part of the information Professor Baldwin brought up from Tantamon Four. I don't feel right about erasing it."

Wesley said, "The virus in our computer is only a copy of what's still on the infowafer, isn't it?"

"Maybe," said La Forge. "But the virus has probably been changed by its contact with the Boogeymen and with the *Enterprise* operating programs. Studying those differences might be useful to Lieutenant Shubunkin and Professor Baldwin."

"Ah," said Data. "Very good."

"Then we can't do it?" Wesley said.

"Not without the captain's approval."

"Let's get it, then."

"Right." La Forge touched a companel and said, "Engineering to Captain Picard."

Over the comlink came a hiss of static and Boogey-men singing a primitive chant that Wesley could not understand.

Wesley said, "I don't think we're going to get any help from the usual places."

"No," said La Forge. "The Boogeymen are taking our ship away from us a little piece at a time. It's like being nibbled to death by ducks."

They all were pretty whipped. Even Data looked grim. Wesley had an idea he was sure was in everyone's mind. He suspected that none of them liked it any more than he did. But it had to be said out loud and nobody else seemed willing to say it. He said, "Maybe we should simplify the interface codes and do all the rest of it without the captain's approval."

"Not until we're sure we can't find him," La Forge said.

"It's a big ship," Wesley reminded him.

After a moment of thinking about exactly how big the *Enterprise* was, Data said, "Perhaps the tricorders can be of use."

"Limited range," La Forge said.

"I believe I have solved that problem," Data said

and went on to explain how they could use the *Enterprise*'s onboard sensor net as an antenna.

"Still," La Forge said, "Captain Picard is just one more human male."

"Perhaps," said Data, "but I know his insignia identity code."

"You don't just happen to know that," Wesley said.

"Indeed not. I know the insignia identity code of everyone on the ship."

"Figures," La Forge said. "Go on. How will we use the tricorder and the ship's sensor net?"

La Forge and Wesley listened with growing enthusiasm as Data spoke. By the time he finished they were ready to try his plan. Ten minutes later Data had made the necessary tricorder modifications, and they went to the nearest turbolift. The doors would not open. La Forge tried to override, and after a few false starts the doors opened all the way, but still no one entered the car.

La Forge said, "I hate it when I can't trust my own technology."

"Yeah," said Wesley. "We could end up anywhere."

"The gangway is the only answer," Data said.

La Forge and Wesley agreed morosely. The main engineering section was near the keel of the engineering hull. The captain was almost certain to be above them. After the kind of day he'd had, Wesley did not look forward to a long climb. Yet there seemed to be no alternative. "Let's get to it," he said.

La Forge opened the manual lock, and they looked into the dim stairwell.

"Which way?" said Wesley, though he already knew the answer.

"Up," said Data as he studied the tricorder.

The three of them started climbing.

The holodeck became warmer from the heat rolling in through the open doorway. Nothing could be done about it short of closing the doors, and Picard had decided against attempting that. He had no guarantee the doors would open again. All he could do was request that Pilgrim discontinue the campfire, and he did.

Baldwin had finally stopped laughing maniacally, but he still looked like a bundle of rags and he still chuckled to himself occasionally, then fell into despondency again.

Worf and Ensign Perry returned with Dr. Crusher and Counselor Troi. All of them were dripping wet, and before Picard could ask Worf to report, Dr. Crusher said, "It's raining down there, Captain."

"Where? On deck twelve?" Picard said with surprise.

"Cats and dogs, sir," Ensign Perry said.

"None of us will dissolve," Worf said, but he did not sound happy.

"Where's my patient?" Dr. Crusher said.

They showed her Professor Baldwin, and after a brief stare at Pilgrim, Dr. Crusher set to work with her medical tricorder. She said, "He's under a great deal of stress, but nothing systemic is wrong with him. A shot of lidox will relax him, but in his condition it will probably also put him to sleep."

Picard said, "We need to talk with him now, Doctor. Counselor?"

Troi looked at Baldwin warily and said, "I can no more force him to relax than you can, Captain."

"Do what you can, Counselor. A miracle would be convenient, but I don't expect one. I want to have a rational conversation with Professor Baldwin."

Troi stood where the campfire had been and talked to Baldwin. It was soothing talk, but talk was all she did. Picard thought she was wasting her time, but Baldwin stopped chuckling, and his empty expression was replaced by a small smile. Then Troi knelt before him and held him the way Picard had seen her hold the little blond girl in sickbay. She hugged him and rocked him, all the time cooing into his ear. This was obviously a private moment, and watching it made Picard uncomfortable. Still, he watched. He had to speak with Baldwin as soon as he was able. The Boogeymen took over more of the ship all the time.

After a few moments, Baldwin began to cry. Heavy sobs came and then steady crying and then sniffles. Troi patted him on the back, and he gently pushed her away. She sat back on her heels and watched him.

"Eric," Picard said.

Baldwin looked up at him. He seemed tired, but the madness that had forced everything else from his face was gone. He said, "Yes, Jean-Luc?"

Picard said, "Thank you, Counselor. You gave me a miracle after all." She stood and went to watch from behind Riker. Picard sat in his overstuffed chair and said, "Eric, the combination of the Boogeyman program and the d'Ort'd virus has very nearly taken over the *Enterprise*."

"Ah," Baldwin said without surprise.

"How did you modify the d'Ort'd program? They don't seem to know."

"You've spoken with the d'Ort'd?"

"Yes. Pilgrim here is their representative."

While Baldwin looked at him, Pilgrim said, "The d'Ort'd greet you, Baldwin. You must give what help you can or we are all doomed."

"Yes. Of course." He looked at Picard and said, "The d'Ort'd speak through this?"

"For lack of a better phrase, the d'Ort'd are a computer program," Riker said. "They've created this persona for our convenience."

"Amazing," Baldwin said quietly. "And Shubunkin thought we would understand them in two weeks." He shook his head.

"Eric," Picard said, "we must know."

"Right." He seemed to gather his thoughts and then said, "I'm not a computer specialist, but being alone on most of my expeditions I learned a few things for my own amusement." He smiled. It was the old winning smile. Picard could not help smiling back.

"I did not know that the d'Ort'd were the program I found on the teardrop ship. I thought the program was just an artifact."

Pilgrim did not react to this. He answered questions, but Picard never saw him express an emotion.

Baldwin said, "Anyway, I saw that I could use the program. All I had to do was insert my name into the matrix. I worked for three weeks figuring out how."

"Not bad for a man who isn't a specialist," Riker said.

"I do okay. The modified d'Ort'd program was on a

secured sector of the infowafer. No one could access it except me."

"Then you did install it in our computer banks on purpose," Picard said.

"Yes. When I first came on board I intended to wait till we got to Memory Alpha to install it. Commander Mont's attack changed my mind. I saw that I could no longer wait. Have you transmitted any messages to Starfleet lately?"

"No," said Riker. "Go on."

Baldwin pleaded with Picard. "You must send a message. Any message. It will contain the virus. I can start to disappear."

"Not while the Boogeymen are still active."

Baldwin tried to speak, but Picard continued. "And even if the Boogeymen were not a problem, I would not allow your name to be deleted from Federation records. You are a part of Federation history, and neither of us has the authority to change that." He shook his head. "I'm not certain that anybody does."

"Fame is a poor substitute for a good night's sleep."

The room was silent but damned hot. Only Worf seemed to be entirely at ease. Worf and Pilgrim. If it got much hotter, some of the more delicate machinery would begin to break down. If it got much hotter, they would parboil in their uniforms.

"Eric," Picard said finally. "You must tell us how you modified the d'Ort'd code. It's the only way we'll be able to untangle them from the Boogeymen."

Baldwin threw his hands up in despair. "Jean-Luc, it took me three weeks to figure out what to change and how to do it. I think it would take me at least that long to delete what I did." His gaze met Picard's. "I'm sorry."

Picard sighed heavily.

"Right back where we started," said Riker.

Picard laid a hand on Baldwin's shoulder, then turned to Worf, and said, "Can you set that tricorder to look for Data? Perhaps he and Mr. La Forge will have some ideas."

"Yes, sir." Worf took the tricorder back from Riker and glared at it as he pushed buttons.

Picard stood up. "Well, then, gentlemen, I suggest—"

"Captain," Worf interrupted. "Data is moving toward us along the gangway in the secondary hull."

Riker said, "If they'd found a solution they wouldn't be coming just to tell us about it. They'd have implemented it by now."

"Indeed. They must have something else in mind. Mr. Perry, as ranking command officer, it is your responsibility to look out for Professor Baldwin's safety."

Perry nodded. "Yes, sir. I assume that Dr. Crusher and Counselor Troi will be staying here with us?"

"Unless they have business elsewhere," Picard said.

Dr. Crusher said, "With the comlink down, house calls seem unlikely."

"I suspect," Troi said carefully, "that the need is greatest here."

"Very well. Number One? Mr. Worf?"

They marched to the corridor, where the air seemed hotter than it had been—more like soup than stuff to breathe. Picard crossed the corridor and went into the stairwell, where the air was considerably cooler. But he suddenly felt heavier.

"Gravity is up," Worf said.

"Warrior's gravity," Riker said. To which Worf only growled.

"Lead on, Mr. Worf."

Worf nodded and descended, sweeping his tricorder before him.

"There's the hatch to deck seventeen," La Forge said and sat down heavily at the top of the flight of stairs.

Wesley sank next to him, and said, "I feel like I've put on a lot of weight since we started." At first the exercise had been invigorating, but after the first few flights, Wesley got bored. He did cube roots in his head to keep awake.

"Gravity is our friend, Wes. We're just tired."

"You may be tired, Geordi, but Wesley's feelings are correct. The gravity gradient is up seven point three percent. Of course, our mass is still the same."

La Forge struggled to his feet and opened an access panel on the wall. He touched a control surface and shook his head. "The Boogeymen have everything all bollixed up." He slammed the access panel closed and sat down next to Wesley.

Data swept the tricorder around and said, "The captain is on his way here."

"Here?" Wesley said.

"In our direction."

Did the captain know something he wanted to tell them, or did he hope they had something to tell *him?*

"Where is he?" La Forge said.

"Deck thirteen and traveling."

La Forge stood up, blinked, and shook his head. "It's not fair to feel this heavy without having eaten something wonderful first."

Wesley stood up more carefully than La Forge had and said, "Gravity is our friend, Geordi."

La Forge gave Wesley a dirty look and began climbing. He said, "If we keep moving we ought to meet him around deck fifteen." He took a step, and his foot was still in the air when the stairwell tilted, throwing all of them into the hatch to deck seventeen. They lay in a heap in a trough made by the hatch and the landing before it; the staircase they'd just ascended now looked like a corrugated floor.

As they sought to untangle themselves, Wesley heard a roar. "What's that?" He had to shout to be heard.

"Air recyclers," said Data.

Wesley and La Forge began to gasp.

"Can't . . ." La Forge said and then collapsed.

Red blotches appeared before Wesley's eyes, and a pounding in his ears blotted out the hurricane whoosh of the air recyclers. The last thing he remembered before he passed out was Data shaking him by the shoulders and asking him if he was all right.

Chapter Fifteen

PICARD AWOKE with an environmental mask over his face. The stuff he was breathing had an odd smell, but Starfleet put the smell into emergency air canisters on purpose, and he knew it would not hurt him.

The last thing he remembered was gasping for breath on the gangway between decks thirteen and fourteen. He had a vague impression that Mr. Worf had carried him to where he now lay. If that was true, he had probably also put the environmental mask on him.

The Boogeymen were becoming stronger. Picard was certain they had it within their power to destroy the *Enterprise* at this moment, if only they knew how. Wesley had designed them to be crafty and merciless, but evidently they needed time to absorb information from the main computer. Of course, an invulnerable and omnipotent enemy would be no more interesting to fight than one you could defeat without trying.

Lucky for them all that the Boogeymen were not perfect.

Deck fourteen was a residential section, and crew members were sprawled all around Picard. Others moved among them, making them more comfortable. They all wore environmental masks, which made them look a little sinister, like Borg insects, perhaps.

Enterprise's designers had been wise to make the availability of emergency masks a function of pressure rather than of the computer. A loss of pressure caused the ceiling canisters to open and let the masks drop. It was an entirely mechanical process and therefore not under the control of the Boogeymen.

Picard stood up, a little shakily at first, and asked an ensign where Mr. Worf and Commander Riker were. The ensign had no idea. Neither did the lieutenant Picard asked next. In the confusion caused by the catastrophic pressure drop it would be easy to lose a person or two. Picard decided to wait where he was. Riker and Worf were sure to return. He walked up and down the corridor, peeked into rooms to make sure the occupants were all right, offered words of comfort where he could.

There was much curiosity, but no hysteria, no panic. Picard was proud of his people.

He was explaining about the Boogeymen and the d'Ort'd to a small crowd of crew members when Riker and Worf returned. With them were La Forge, Data, and Wesley.

"We found them on deck seventeen," Worf said as if he'd found his missing socks at last.

La Forge said, "We were coming to meet you, sir. Then everything went black."

"We experienced a sudden and dangerous pressure drop," Data said. "It was fortunate that the pressure drop was the same both on deck seventeen and on the gangway. Otherwise I never would have gotten the hatch open and gained access to the environmental masks."

"Data saved our lives," Wesley said, obviously pleased.

"That is quite probably true," Data said.

"When we have time to give commendations, Mr. Data shall receive one. So shall you all. But right now I hope you have good news for me."

"Maybe, Captain," La Forge said.

The deck began to roll like the deck of an ocean-going vessel. "More gravity fluctuations," Data said.

"And," said Worf, "the temperature is dropping."

"Report, Mr. La Forge," Riker said.

"Yes, sir. Data suggested that if we simplify the interface codes between input and the mainframe's first lobe, a machete program would be able to delete the Boogeyman-d'Ort'd virus."

"You mean the entire program, not just the Boogeyman part of it."

"Yes, sir."

Riker and Picard frowned. Worf's expression was unreadable. Riker said, "We could still send the original d'Ort'd program back to the teardrop on Tantamon Four."

"Absolutely," said La Forge.

"I'm afraid you don't understand," Picard said. "The d'Ort'd program in our computer is not just an artifact of an alien culture. It embodies the aliens themselves." It was definitely getting colder. Picard wondered how long that would matter.

"You mean," said Wesley, "the d'Ort'd race is a computer program?" La Forge and Data shared his amazement.

La Forge said, "When we have a little free time, I'd like somebody to explain that."

Wesley shook his head. "For the purposes of the machete program it doesn't matter if the d'Ort'd are a race or a computer program or what. We can erase the Boogeymen-d'Ort'd combination and then send the original infowafer d'Ort'd back to Tantamon Four."

Data said, "The problem is not that simple, Wesley. The original in Worf's safe would have no knowledge of anything the d'Ort'd program experienced aboard *Enterprise.*"

"Yes," said Picard, "and such knowledge would certainly be useful if the Federation and the d'Ort'd are ever to understand each other." In his own mind Picard was weighing the importance of good Federation-d'Ort'd relations against the safety of his ship. Ultimately, if the *Enterprise* was destroyed, both updated and original d'Ort'd programs would be destroyed with it, benefiting nobody. Only the copy in the teardrop on Tantamon IV would still exist, and it would have no knowledge of *Enterprise* or of the Federation. Picard could choose to save the *Enterprise* or to save nothing at all.

Still, to destroy an entire race, or even a copy of an entire race, was horrible. All his Starfleet training, including the *Kobayashi Maru* scenario, had not prepared him to make such a monumental decision.

Picard said, "How long would it take you to implement your plan?"

La Forge said, "If Data's calculations are correct—and they always are—about fifteen minutes."

Picard glanced at Riker, who was watching him, waiting for the word, probably not envying him this decision. The captain said, "Very well. Mr. Data, do everything you must, right up to the point where you activate the machete program. You will do that only on my command."

"Aye, sir. Given the current state of the *Enterprise,* I believe that I will have greater success if I input the new interface codes directly instead of through a terminal."

"Right you are, Mr. Data. Be careful." Picard smiled. "And please send everyone on holodeck three my regards."

Riker said, "I think, given the condition of our comlink, we should all stay together so we can coordinate our efforts."

"Very good, Number One. Mr. La Forge, Mr. Crusher, you have the more difficult but, in the end, more satisfying task."

"I know, sir," said La Forge. "You want us to look for a way to untangle the Boogeymen from the d'Ort'd."

"You must keep trying till the last possible moment."

"Aye, sir. What is it, Wes?"

Wesley seemed reluctant to speak, so Picard said, "What is it, Mr. Crusher? We have no time for delicacy."

"We can't just untangle the Boogeymen from the d'Ort'd. Without the d'Ort'd influence holding them back, the Boogeymen will carry out their prime function, which is to destroy the *Enterprise.*"

Picard looked inquisitively at La Forge.

La Forge said, "Then we'll just have to find a way to erase the Boogeymen before we free the d'Ort'd. A snap for a couple of geniuses like us."

Worf taking point, they left for the stairwell, rolling with the deck like sailors on a water ship.

Holodeck three was hot, as was all of deck eleven. Professor Baldwin, Ensign Perry, Dr. Crusher, and Counselor Troi sat in the overstuffed chairs facing each other and sweating large dark spots into their clothes. They spoke in low, confidential tones, conserving energy, not wanting to exert themselves till exertion became necessary. Nearby stood Pilgrim, the holodeck persona of the d'Ort'd. He did not sweat, did not blink, did not move, did not show any interest in the discussion.

"It must be cooler somewhere else," Dr. Crusher said.

"I'd hate to think this was the coolest place on the ship," Ensign Perry said.

Troi was fanning herself with one hand. She said, "We can't go anywhere else. The captain will look for us here."

"Wouldn't want to disappoint the captain," Baldwin said.

"I have a feeling," Dr. Crusher said, "you've already disappointed the captain."

"How's that?"

"He wouldn't say."

"Good old honorable Jean-Luc."

After a long silence during which nothing moved but Troi's hand and drops of sweat, Troi said, "Why don't you tell us about it?" Baldwin gave no sign that he'd heard her. She added, "Just to help pass the time."

No one else said anything so after a while Baldwin began to speak. He started with his washing out of Starfleet Academy, an event that he now seemed to find humorous, and then told them how he'd entered the University of Syrtis Major on Mars. He'd made a big name there as a hot-shot exologist who took chances that paid off. After that his career was one adventure after another, with rest periods during which he piled up more honors than any exologist who'd come before him. He became a romantic public figure as well as a scientist.

"And," he said, "I picked up a few enemies. People who were upset that I wanted to work for museums instead of for them. Which brings me to how I disappointed your captain. Are you listening, Pilgrim?"

As usual, Pilgrim said nothing.

Baldwin said, "You all know about the Boogeyman-d'Ort'd virus?"

"I don't," Ensign Perry said.

"According to Captain Picard, it's the computer program that's responsible for the breakdown of the *Enterprise.*"

"We cannot stop the Boogeymen," Pilgrim said, surprising everyone.

"You're not alone," Baldwin said. "Anyway, I

brought the d'Ort'd program on board not only to study but to use as a tool that would remove my name from all Federation records."

"Why?" said Troi.

"I assume you want to know why I would want to remove my name, not why I brought the program on board. Remember Commander Mont? He was not my only enemy. I wanted to disappear. Let my enemies chase one another for a change."

"And?" said Dr. Crusher darkly.

"And somehow the d'Ort'd program got out of hand. Somehow the Boogeyman program hooked up with it and began to take over the ship."

Dr. Crusher said, "You're responsible for the condition of the ship?"

"You see," said Baldwin. "Now I've gone and disappointed you, too."

Ensign Perry had her face scrunched up in thought. Whatever she was thinking about, she was still working it through when she said, "So you used this d'Ort'd program to erase your name from Federation records?"

"Right."

"And now you'd like to erase this Boogeyman program, but save the d'Ort'd program."

"Right," said Dr. Crusher. "But nobody can pry them apart."

While Ensign Perry thought some more, Troi said, "I have an idea."

Baldwin smiled. "I didn't know you were a computer expert, too."

"I'm not—but then, neither were you," Troi pointed out.

"What is it, Deanna?" Dr. Crusher asked, somewhat impatiently.

"Well . . . why not replace the Professor Baldwin reference string, which Eric put in the d'Ort'd program, with the Boogeyman program? That way, instead of searching for and erasing Professor Baldwin, the d'Ort'd program will search for and erase the Boogeymen."

Baldwin sat up straight, his eyes wide with astonishment. "That's absolutely brilliant. Why didn't one of us computer geniuses think of it?"

"The forest for the trees," Dr. Crusher said. "You were looking for a complicated solution."

"What is absolutely brilliant?" Picard said as he and the others walked onto the holodeck.

"Captain," Ensign Perry said and stood up.

"We didn't expect to see you so soon," Dr. Crusher said.

Riker said, "We're on our way to deck ten to try out the various solutions La Forge and his team have come up with."

"None of them seem perfect," La Forge said.

Baldwin said, "Counselor Troi has a good idea."

With a little encouragement from Picard, Troi explained her proposal. Picard and Riker nodded. La Forge, Data, and Wesley seemed to be struck dumb with amazement. Troi tried hard not to show how pleased she was, but a satisfied smile broke through her composure.

Data, the first to recover, said, "It is quite elegant."

"It'll work," La Forge said.

"Pretty good," Wesley admitted, obviously unhappy about something.

Dr. Crusher said, "Give yourself a break, Wesley."

"Yeah." Wesley finally smiled, too.

La Forge said, "How would you like a job down in Engineering, Counselor?"

Troi looked embarrassed and Picard said, "I assure you, Mr. La Forge, Counselor Troi is much too valuable to me up on the bridge. Pilgrim, how does the search-and-replace idea seem to you?"

"We will fight the Boogeymen this way."

"That sounds like agreement to me," Riker said. "I suggest we stop congratulating ourselves and get to work."

"Indeed," said Picard. "Shall we all adjourn to deck ten?"

Picard was happy to get back into the stairwell where it was cool. His people streamed out behind him as they mounted the stairs, a little optimism in the air for a change. He was on a landing, ready to climb the final staircase to deck ten when the emergency Klaxon began to whoop.

"Red alert, red alert," a Boogeyman cried. "All lifeboats away!"

As the sound of lifeboats being ejected into space pounded through the walls, Picard shouted, "Mr. La Forge!"

La Forge was already at an access box punching in codes while Data and Wesley looked over his shoulder. They were still at it when a Boogeyman cried, "All airlocks, arm explosive bolts. Prepare for emergency jettison! All isolating hatches open! Five minutes by my mark!"

"Override, Mr. La Forge," Riker shouted.

La Forge turned to him and said, "Override impossible, sir. The Boogeymen have hatch and airlock control routed in such a way that we can't override without shutting down the warp engines' antimatter containment fields."

"We're doomed either way," Wesley said.

Worf nodded. "It is a good day to die."

"Mark!" said the Boogeyman and immediately began the five-minute countdown. Another Boogeyman cried, "We win! We win!"

Chapter Sixteen

"COME ON," said Picard as he bounded up the stairs. He could not pull the hatch open. "Jammed," he said.

Worf and Data tried together to open it, and at last, with a creak and a groan from the hatch, they succeeded.

The Klaxon continued, and the Boogeyman announced calmly, "Four minutes twenty seconds and counting."

Picard set his fingertips against the blue panel outside the computer core control center. It seemed to take forever before the computer, using the voice of a Boogeyman, said, "Ensign Jean-Luc Picard is not cleared for this area."

Everybody but Picard, Data, and Wesley was astonished by this.

"Mr. Crusher," Picard said, trying to keep calm.

Wesley stepped forward and set his fingertips

against the ID panel. "Captain Wesley Crusher is identified," the Boogeyman said.

"Open control center," Wesley said.

"Three minutes fifty seconds," a Boogeyman said and laughed.

"Clearance confirmed," another Boogeyman said, and the doors slid open. The security field went down with a snap.

Everyone gathered inside. La Forge studied the schematic of *Enterprise*'s computer system and said, "What a mess."

"Mr. Data?" Riker said.

Data stood poised next to the proper port, cable in hand. He said, "Given the constraints under which we are working, I think it best for me to input Counselor Troi's changes directly."

Dr. Crusher said, "Last time you tried that you got the flu."

"He was in passive mode last time," La Forge said.

"Still," Picard said, "what Mr. Data suggests is dangerous."

"Three minutes thirty seconds and counting."

Data said, "We really do not have the time to argue."

"Make it so," Picard said.

Using the cable, Data plugged himself into the port, and his eyes began to move as if he were zip-scanning a book.

"Abort airlock jettison sequence," Picard shouted. He did not have much faith his order would be obeyed, but there was nothing else to do.

"Three minutes twenty seconds and counting."

"Try it, Wesley," Picard said.

"Abort airlock jettison sequence."

For a moment it seemed as if Wesley had succeeded, and then the Boogeyman said, "Three minutes ten seconds and counting."

"Come on, Data," Dr. Crusher said.

Picard wanted to say the same thing though he knew such encouragement was pointless. Events moved slowly. Hours came and went between ten-second calls.

"There minutes."

Data continued to input the program changes. The others concentrated on him as if their thoughts and wishes could make his job go faster, ensure its success.

"Two minutes fifty seconds."

"Abort airlock jettison sequence," Picard commanded.

"Two minutes forty seconds."

"Abort airlock jettison sequence," Wesley said.

The countdown and the Klaxon continued. Data worked.

"Two minutes," the Boogeyman said and laughed.

Data pulled the cable from the port and from his head and said, "The Boogeyman reference string is installed."

"There goes the d'Ort'd virus," La Forge said and pointed to a small magnifying glass symbol leaping from place to place on the schematic, leaving behind replicas of itself. It flashed and moved on. Picard knew that parts of the computer did not have to call on the modified virus program to make it spread. It would go where the Boogeyman-d'Ort'd program was already in place. As fast as it was, the process seemed painfully slow.

"Will it work fast enough?" Wesley said.

"Will it work at all?" La Forge said.

"One minute fifty seconds."

At one minute, Picard gave the abort order again. Then Wesley gave it. They tried every ten seconds thereafter.

"Thirty seconds to emergency airlock jettison," a Boogeyman said and laughed.

Chapter Seventeen

WE ARE ALL GOING TO DIE, Picard thought calmly. The mysterious force that Riker claimed watched over ships called *Enterprise* had failed at last. And no one would ever know why. Someday a Federation starship would come out to Tantamon IV to investigate *Enterprise*'s disappearance. They would find wreckage, evidence of an antimatter breech, and absolutely no clue as to why this had happened. Nothing they found on the planet would help them. Picard could not even send a helpful message without contaminating every computer in the Federation.

That was all right. The Federation did not need warning—though the mystery of the lost *Enterprise* would probably be the subject of cocktail party talk for months. It was unlikely such a tragedy would occur again. Without the unhappy coincidental meeting of the d'Ort'd, Baldwin's desire to disappear, and

Wesley's Boogeymen, this tragedy would not have happened even once. So much for Riker's mysterious force.

"Twenty seconds to emergency jettison."

Picard's people were taking it well. Perhaps they could not comprehend the enormity of the tragedy. One could imagine the death of loved ones, perhaps even one's own death. But it was more difficult to believe the death of one's entire universe.

"Ten seconds to emergency jettison."

"Abort sequence," Picard said. Wesley repeated the command.

"Sequence aborted," said the normal computer voice.

At first Picard thought he'd heard wrong. Then he thought this must be another Boogeyman trick: give the dullards hope, then snatch it away from them.

But the Klaxon had stopped. Gravity was normal. Temperature seemed to be returning to normal. The only sounds he heard were the hiss of the air recyclers and the small movements of the people around him.

"Is it over?" Ensign Perry said.

Picard said, "Apparently so."

Perry started to cry with relief, and Troi comforted her. They all comforted one another. With some embarrassment, Picard found himself hugging Dr. Crusher. He patted her on the back and pulled away. She smiled at him. He gave her back a quick professional smile and turned to watch La Forge and Data study the schematic and point things out to each other. Then La Forge sat down at one of the terminals and began to type.

While watching the schematic, Data said, "Interlocks now in place and functioning normally."

"Technology," said La Forge. "I love it."

Picard said, "Thank you, Mr. Data, Mr. La Forge, Mr. Crusher. Thank you all. Every one of you contributed to our success."

Wesley said, "I guess the Boogeymen didn't win after all."

"You needn't sound so smug, Mr. Crusher," Picard said. "It was a very near thing for us."

"Yes, sir."

Riker said, "How does it look, La Forge?"

"All systems apparently nominal, sir."

"Apparently?"

"According to the instruments," La Forge said.

Riker did not appear pleased with this answer, but he said no more.

"What about the d'Ort'd?" Baldwin said.

La Forge said, "Computer, what is the condition of Pilgrim, the d'Ort'd persona on holodeck three?"

"Program running."

"Continue program," Picard said. "Let's find out if systems are nominal in reality as well as in appearance. All bridge personnel please join me on the bridge."

"We're going to take the turbolift, aren't we, sir?" Wesley said, sounding a little worried.

"Have you another suggestion?"

"Uh, no, sir."

Picard said, "The rest of you wait here till we contact you."

"Aye, Captain," La Forge said.

They walked to the turbolift and the doors opened.

All seemed normal, but Riker said, "I suggest that you and I take separate cars."

"If you insist, Number One. Wesley, Mr. Worf."

The three of them got into the car. The doors shushed closed, and Picard said, "Bridge."

The car began to move immediately. The sound and smooth ride seemed normal to Picard. He smiled at Worf and Wesley. They nodded back, but without confidence. The car slowed and stopped, and the doors opened onto the bridge. On the viewscreen, Tantamon IV turned placidly. Worf and Wesley seemed surprised they had arrived at the right place, and the truth was, Picard was surprised himself, though pleased.

Picard found Ensign Winston-Smyth pacing. "Sir!" she cried when she saw Picard and Worf and Wesley, and ran toward them. Her joy at seeing Picard again was obviously real, but he was certain her feelings were more professional than personal. An ensign could be no more comfortable commanding the bridge—even if the Boogeymen made the job largely honorary—than Picard had been asking her to do it.

"Anything to report, Ensign?" Picard said.

"The life craft are all gone, sir, but we still have our airlocks in place."

"That's the spirit," Picard said. "Ensign, you are relieved."

"Thank you, sir." Winston-Smyth walked quickly to the turbolift. The doors opened and Riker got out with Data and Troi. The ensign ducked into the turbolift and was gone.

"No adventures I trust, Number One?"

"None, sir."

Picard raised his voice and said, "Mr. La Forge?"

"Here, sir."

"Please escort Professor Baldwin to holodeck three and wait for me there."

"Aye, sir."

"Dr. Crusher, it is safe for you to return to sickbay. Ensign Perry, return to your post."

Perry and Dr. Crusher acknowledged, and Picard said to Riker, "Much more convenient than running messages through the gangway."

"Yes, sir."

"Lieutenant Shubunkin," Picard called.

"Is that you, Captain?" Shubunkin said over the comlink.

"Indeed it is, Lieutenant. Please meet me on holodeck three."

"Is that possible, sir?"

"It is. Please comply."

"Aye, sir."

"Number One, you have the bridge."

"Aye, sir."

"Ensign Crusher, please join me."

Wesley beamed as the two of them got onto the turbolift. He said, "Sir, I'd like to try the Boogeyman program mark two."

"You do not astonish me, Ensign."

"Yes, sir. Do I have your permission?"

Picard knew he could not deny Wesley permission to experiment with the holodeck any more than he could deny an experiment to someone in his science section. Besides, it was not the young man's fault that he had timed his first Boogeyman experiment to coincide with the arrival of Professor Baldwin's doctored alien program. Picard said, "Permission granted."

Wesley smiled and said, "Thank you, sir."

They rode without incident to deck eleven. Air temperature and gravity seemed normal. Inside holodeck three Picard and Wesley found the same four overstuffed chairs along with Baldwin, La Forge, and a godlike being dressed in a pirate outfit. The being was tall and bronze and handsome. He had the noble bearing of someone who knew he had nothing to prove. Picard approached the being and said, "Pilgrim?"

"Yes."

"You look different."

"The Boogeymen are gone."

"Yes. We can send you back to your ship aboard the infowafer."

"We cannot leave. We have no pusher."

Picard turned to Baldwin. "Eric," he said, "you asked me to erase your name from Federation records. I can't do that. But I am not without sympathy for your situation. For this reason, I make you a counterproposal. The d'Ort'd need a pusher—a crew member to accelerate their teardrop ship to warp speed. They cannot return home without one."

"You suggest I go with them?"

Picard said, "Is that such a dreadful alternative? Why did you go to the transporter room when you were running, if not to escape?"

After a moment of consideration Baldwin admitted, "Maybe you're right."

Picard said, "Realize, Eric, that I make this proposal not entirely for your benefit. I hope you will return to Federation space someday and teach us to train our own pushers."

While Baldwin considered, Picard went on. "You are also the perfect choice to be our goodwill ambassador to the d'Ort'd."

"You can't make me an ambassador, Jean-Luc."

"Not officially, no. But I can strongly suggest it."

Baldwin didn't say anything.

"I know what it is, Eric. You don't like running out in the middle of a fight."

"That," Baldwin admitted, "and also, I'm only human. If I go with the d'Ort'd, it'll be a long time before I see another one of my own kind."

"Don't go, then."

"The d'Ort'd can't get home without me."

"Another moral dilemma," Picard said.

"Baldwin must come," Pilgrim said.

While they waited to see what Baldwin's decision would be, Shubunkin arrived, a little breathless. "Everything works," he said with some surprise.

Baldwin said, "Shubunkin, how would you like to take my place on Memory Alpha?"

"It would make my career."

"Jean-Luc, call Starfleet and see if they'll go for it. Why shouldn't Shubunkin make some enemies of his own?"

Shubunkin blanched, but Baldwin smiled broadly.

"You've decided to go?" Picard said.

"Talk about moral dilemmas. After causing everybody so much trouble I guess I have to go."

"You have to go," Pilgrim said.

Picard said, "Computer, discontinue and save d'Ort'd program."

The computer gave its auditory twinkle, and Pilgrim and his chairs disappeared. Except for living beings, the holodeck was now empty. Shubunkin stared at the space where Pilgrim had stood. "That was a d'Ort'd?"

Baldwin put a hand on Shubunkin's shoulder and said, "Lieutenant, it's a lot more complicated than that."

Picard said, "Mr. La Forge, record the d'Ort'd on two infowafers. We will beam one of them down to Tantamon Four with Professor Baldwin; the other is for Lieutenant Shubunkin to study on Memory Alpha."

"Aye, sir." La Forge left.

Wesley said, "What about me, sir?"

"You were present at the beginning, Mr. Crusher. I thought it only fair that you be present at the end."

"Thank you, sir."

"And, Ensign Crusher?"

"Yes, sir?"

"Next time you see fit to install an unorthodox program in the computer, make sure it can't get loose."

"Yes, sir."

Later, back on the bridge, Shubunkin stood next to Counselor Troi taking everything in, not nearly so arrogant as he'd been when Picard first met him. The captain thought he might be considering what Baldwin had said about making enemies.

Picard said, "Transporter room two."

"Here, Captain. Professor Baldwin is ready."

"Good-bye, Professor," Shubunkin said. "Looks as if you are going on another great adventure."

"I guess it's kind of a habit," Baldwin said good-naturedly.

"Good luck, Eric," Picard said. "I look forward to your report."

"So do I. Let's get this over with. And don't let Counselor Troi say good-bye to me, or I'll change my mind and stay."

Troi's mouth twitched and almost became a smile, but she said nothing.

"Energize," Picard said.

After Baldwin was on the planet, *Enterprise* stayed in orbit around Tantamon IV for almost half an hour. During that time Picard thought about what his ship had just been through; but now that the excitement was over, his mind kept returning to the Dixon Hill scenario and to Rhonda Howe. He wondered if she had been flushed from the system along with Wesley's Boogeymen.

Troi interrupted his thoughts, saying, "I feel it, the same way I felt when I went into the warp trance, but different too, less frantic."

Data, at Ops, said, "Teardrop ship taking off, sir."

"On visual," Riker said.

The teardrop ship rose around the curve of Tantamon IV. Sensors followed it for a moment, and then it was gone.

Wesley said, "It's there and then it isn't."

"Warp without warp drive," Shubunkin said.

"We will have to make do the old-fashioned way," Picard said. "Best speed for Memory Alpha."

"Aye, Captain," said Wesley. He was grateful that at warp eight the *Enterprise* would not take two weeks to get there, but it was still a milk run.

When his watch was over, Wesley went down to see Ensign Winston-Smyth. She was not in her cabin, giving him cause to be grateful that the computer was up again; he would never have known where to look for her if it hadn't been. He found her in Ten Forward sitting by herself in a dim corner of the room sipping a sunny yellow drink that had a paper parasol in it.

"Ensign?" said Wesley.

She looked up at him and tried to smile welcome, but he could see it was an effort. Her face had no more expression than an empty petri dish.

"May I sit down?"

Winston-Smyth sighed and pulled herself together. She flashed Wesley a real smile and said, "I guess I can't go off line forever."

Wesley sat down and watched her sip her drink. Beyond her the warp eight star rainbows arced across the windows. He said, "What was it like?"

"What?"

"Being in command of the *Enterprise.*"

At first Winston-Smyth seemed not to know what Wesley meant. Then she shook her head and said, "I wasn't any more in command than someone riding an amusement planet adventure."

"You had the bridge to yourself."

Winston-Smyth sighed again and said, "It was pretty scary, Wesley."

"The Boogeymen. I know."

"No, actually I was kind of glad they were running things. When they vanished all of a sudden, I had no idea what to do." She sipped her drink. "Kind of makes me wonder if I'm in the right racket."

"It wasn't a fair test. Captain Picard left you in command only because there was no one else to do the job."

"Yeah, but still . . ."

"You know," said Wesley, "Captain Picard was an ensign himself a long time ago."

"Meaning?"

"Meaning a long time from now, *you'll* be ready to be a captain."

Winston-Smyth shrugged. "Maybe," she said.

"Yeah, maybe." This entire conversation reminded Wesley of the one he'd had with Geordi back when they'd first discussed the Borders scale and Boogeymen. Only this time, Wesley was the one giving the sage advice. He said, "You'll know when you're ready. Starfleet doesn't give out Galaxy-class starships like lollipops."

The observation seemed to please her. It pleased Wesley, too, because he knew he was right, just as Geordi had been right. Wesley didn't need Boogeymen or the Starfleet training programs at the moment. In good time he'd go to the Academy and move up through the ranks, and when Starfleet Command gave him his own ship he'd be ready for it. He took a certain amount of comfort in knowing that wiser heads were watching over him.

With the heavy stuff out of the way, Wesley had time to notice that Ensign Winston-Smyth was not just a fellow officer but a pretty young woman. Just thinking about turning their meeting into a social encounter made Wesley sweat. But he would never forgive himself if he lost this opportunity.

He said, "What's that you're drinking, Barbara?"

"A Vulcan Sunrise. It's good."

"I'll have one, too."

After that, Wesley and Ensign Winston-Smyth talked for a long time. They started by discussing what it took to be a good commander, but as happens in good conversations, the topic wandered.

When Picard's watch was over he went to his cabin and had his clothing slot stitch up Dixon Hill's brown double-breasted suit and fedora. When he got to holodeck three, Picard said, "Computer, Dixon Hill scenario involving Rhonda Howe."

Picard held his breath for a moment; then the computer twinkled and said, "Scenario ready." The holodeck opened, showing Dixon Hill's office. Picard could smell the ancient decay of the run-down building and hear the noise of internal combustion traffic.

As he was about to enter, Dr. Crusher hurried up, also dressed in 1940s garb.

"Dr. Crusher, how delightful." Picard didn't really know whether he was delighted or not. He'd hoped to get to know Rhonda Howe better. With Dr. Crusher along, that would be impossible. On the other hand, she looked wonderful in her forties outfit. Perhaps Rhonda Howe would not be necessary.

"I had the computer notify me if you asked for your Dixon Hill clothes. After hearing about Rhonda Howe, I thought you might go back to that scenario when you had the time."

It was only a holodeck scenario, Picard thought. He could run it again if he had to. "Very well, Doctor. Shall we see if we can discover whodunit?" Picard offered his arm to Dr. Crusher and she took it. Together they walked onto the holodeck and into Dixon Hill's office.